On the way back to the Home, we took a bus, just for a change. It takes longer, but it gets us out among ordinary people. You can imagine that no matter how pleasant and friendly are the residents of the Home (and believe me, they aren't always either one), we are all, as they say, of advanced years....

It was going to take some time for us to digest all these new facts, as well as those we already knew and had already told the police, but now had sworn not to reveal. In a way, we were supposed to be helping the police, and at the same time we were also supposed to be helping their chief suspect. They say in Yiddish, *Mit eyn tokhes ken men nit tantsn af tsvey khasenes*.

You can't dance at two weddings with one *tuchis*.

Praise for Mark Reutlinger

Praise for MRS. KAPLAN AND THE MATZOH BALL OF DEATH, first book in this series:

"Is there kosher food in jail? These two heroines have gotten themselves in quite a pickle! Well, it's a matzoh ball mess, really. Too deliciously funny!"

~ Rita Mae Brown,
bestselling author of Nine Lives to Die

"The antics of Rose and Ida had me clutching my sides as I laughed out loud. A hilarious cozy I enjoyed. Fans of Rita Mae Brown and Peter Falk mysteries will love this book".

~ N. N. Light

"A pure joy to read . . . This book oozes with charm, humor and mystery."

~Socrates' Book Reviews

"A hilarious book featuring wonderful characters. Mark Reutlinger is a wonderful writer. His characters come alive on the page (though some drop dead), and they are, in general, excellent company. Treat yourself and read his books."

~ Dana Isaacson, author and editor

Oy Vey, Maria!
A Mrs. Kaplan Mystery

by

Mark Reutlinger

This is a work of fiction. Names, characters, places, and incidents are either the product of the author's imagination or are used fictitiously, and any resemblance to actual persons living or dead, business establishments, events, or locales, is entirely coincidental.

Oy Vey, Maria!, A Mrs. Kaplan Mystery

COPYRIGHT © 2021 by Mark Reutlinger

Cover Art by *Debbie Taylor*

The Wild Rose Press, Inc.
PO Box 708
Adams Basin, NY 14410-0708
Visit us at www.thewildrosepress.com

Publishing History
First Edition, 2021
Trade Paperback ISBN 978-1-5092-3835-4
Digital ISBN 978-1-5092-3836-1

Published in the United States of America

Dedication

To Analee and Elliot, with love.

Acknowledgements

My thanks to my wife and patient beta reader Analee, and to my friends Shelly and Heather, whose descriptions of actual events in their experience are reflected in my story. (The murder, however, is purely fiction.)

There is a very easy way to return from a casino with a small fortune: go there with a large one."

~ *Jack Yelton*

Chapter 1

If I didn't know better, I'd think that whenever it's too quiet here at the Julius and Rebecca Cohen Home for Jewish Seniors, my friend Rose Kaplan gets bored and conjures up a dead body under mysterious circumstances. Then she can make like her hero, Mr. Sherlock Holmes, and solve the mystery.

And I'm not all that certain I know better.

The latest example of this talent of hers began just after breakfast on a sunny day in March. The Home was preparing for the holiday of Purim, when we celebrate Queen Esther saving the Jews in ancient Persia (but more about that later). Mrs. K and I were sitting in the lounge, enjoying the warmth of the morning sun coming through the nearby east window and sipping our tea. Chamomile, I think. It was one of those times when you just want to relax and appreciate the noise and commotion that isn't there. So neither of us was overjoyed when Naomi Schwartz came along and broke the silence.

Now don't get me wrong. Naomi, who lives not far from the Home, is a very nice young lady (well, at our age fiftyish seems pretty young). Not particularly attractive, just what you might call wholesome. But when she starts to talk, any quiet in the immediate neighborhood packs up and goes home. And she can really *hak a chainik.* (It means like banging on a teakettle, which is what it sounded like on that otherwise

1

(peaceful morning.) You know, talk your ear off.

"Good morning, Mrs. Kaplan, Mrs. Berkowitz," she said, a *bissel* louder than necessary. The eyes and ears of those sitting nearby turned our way. "How are you feeling this morning?" Her lips had on them a smile, but somehow her eyes were sending a different message.

"How should we feel?" Mrs. K said. "It's a beautiful day, and we are alive and able to enjoy it." I nodded in agreement.

"Absolutely," Naomi said. "A gorgeous day." But she didn't sound convinced. She was looking down at her shoes, not out the window.

"So, Naomi," Mrs. K said to keep the conversation going, "it is almost Purim. Will you be coming here to our Purim celebration? I assume your mother will be there."

Naomi's mother, Miriam Blumenthal, was one of our oldest residents.

"I suppose so. Actually, Purim was a bit of a downer for me when I was growing up," Naomi said.

"Really?" Mrs. K said. "Why? Purim is usually more fun for children than adults."

"Maybe it was because mother made me participate in the Purim play at Sunday school. She said she did it when she was a kid, even bragged how good an actress she was, insisted I do the same, though I was kind of shy and didn't want to. To make a long story short, I was chosen to be Queen Esther, the best part, but when I was supposed to make my big speech, I forgot my lines. It was so embarrassing, and it kind of spoiled Purim for me after that."

"Well, at least you could enjoy eating the *hamantaschen,*" Mrs. K said.

2

But apparently not.

"You know," Naomi said, "now that you mention it, there were never any *hamantaschen* in the house. It's hard to really celebrate Purim without *hamantaschen*."

This is true. *Hamantaschen,* the three-cornered cookies shaped like the hat of the *nogoodnik* Haman and filled with fruit or poppy seeds, seem to be everywhere at Purim. Even in the *goyisher* bakeries you find them. You don't have to be Jewish to enjoy a nice poppy seed turnover.

After we had exhausted the subject of Purim at the Blumenthal household, Naomi sat on a chair opposite us and leaned closer. Her face had now lost its smile and she looked quite upset. Then she did something she had never done in our presence: She lowered her voice to nearly a whisper.

"I was, uh, was wondering whether you might have a few minutes to talk. In private, I mean," she said as she glanced around the lounge. There were several other residents sitting nearby, and although they all seemed to be reading or just sitting with their eyes closed, perhaps asleep, you can bet bagels to blintzes that anything interesting one of us said would make its way around the Home by evening. And if it was our Mrs. Bissela who was hearing, before lunch.

Mrs. K now looked concerned. "Why, is something wrong? Something about your mother?"

"Yes, but I'd rather not discuss it out here," Naomi said, still in a low voice. "Could we go to your apartment to talk?"

Mrs. K looked over at me and raised her eyebrows as if to say, "This sounds serious."

Ever since Mrs. K gained a reputation for solving

mysteries, residents of the Home and even others have been coming to her and asking for help. It could be anything from finding a lost set of keys to finding out if a murder had been committed, and if so by whom.

Fortunately, Naomi didn't ask us that.

Unfortunately, it was almost as bad.

Chapter 2

Mrs. K and I took a few last sips of our tea and stood up, a *bissel* reluctantly, I will admit.

"*Nu,* come, Naomi," said Mrs. K, "we shall go to my apartment and have a nice talk." She made it sound almost as if she was glad to be leaving her tea and comfy chair, but that's typical of Mrs. K. She always thinks of the other person's feelings before her own. I cannot honestly say I felt quite so charitable, but I didn't want to miss finding out what Naomi had to say that was so secret.

We left the lounge and walked past the foyer and down the hallway to Mrs. K's apartment. On the way we passed Moishe Klein, a nice man who in the past has said he would like to have a "relationship" with me, although I do not wish to have one with him. He smiled and gave me what might have been a wink with his eye. At his age, it's hard to say whether he is winking or suffering from a twitching eyelid, but just in case I simply nodded politely and did not smile (or wink, of course) back, so he shouldn't get the wrong idea.

Once we were safely in Mrs. K's apartment, she asked Naomi to have a seat in the living room. Naomi sat in the pretty beige chair, and Mrs. K and I then sat on the matching sofa opposite her. It is soft and is easy sitting down and sinking in. It's the getting up again that I don't like.

Before Naomi could begin whatever it was she had to say, Mrs. K made the obligatory offer of food. Even bad news goes better with a little *nosh*. "Can I get you something, dear? Some tea or coffee perhaps?"

"Huh? Oh, no, no thank you," Naomi said. She was looking down and squeezing one hand with the other in her lap.

"Then why don't you go ahead and tell us what is the problem. You look completely *fardeiget*," Mrs. K said in a sympathetic tone. And Naomi did indeed look worried.

Naomi looked up at both of us and said, "I'm terribly worried about my mom."

"Why?" Mrs. K asked, sounding concerned. "Has Miriam taken ill? Has she fallen and injured herself?"

I should explain that Naomi's mother spent most of her time in a wheelchair. She could walk a little, like from her bed to her wheelchair, but that was about all. But while Miriam's legs may have been weak, she always seemed to be in good health and spirits, and she seemed to be very close to Naomi and the rest of her family, who visited her often. So when Naomi sounded so distressed about her mother, I suddenly could picture any number of accidents a person unsteady on their feet might suffer.

"Oh no, nothing like that, thank goodness," Naomi replied. "It's about her … her property, I guess you'd say."

"What property is that?" I asked. "Do you mean she has a piece of land somewhere?"

Naomi shook her head. "No," she said, "I mean all of her property … her personal property, and her money."

"Perhaps you should explain," Mrs. K said, as we didn't seem to be making much progress.

"Yes, of course. You see, when it became too difficult for my mom to get around and to do things like bathe and dress herself without help, my brother Barry and I advised her to hire someone to help her."

"Doesn't the Home have people who can help with those things?" I asked. "I know, for example, Mrs. Feinstein down the hall has someone come in when she showers …"

"Yes, I know," Naomi said. "But mom wanted someone who was helping just her, who she could kind of train to do things the way she likes, that sort of thing. And since she has plenty of money, the cost wasn't an issue."

Mrs. K and I nodded. What Naomi was describing is not a common thing to do, but certainly it isn't all that unusual. A place like the Julius and Rebecca Home for Jewish Seniors has only so much help available for the residents, and those wishing more personal attention, and who can afford it, are welcome to employ their own person.

"Anyway, after interviewing several people, mom hired a woman named Maria Cartwright as a sort of full-time companion. You know, not just to help her with dressing and stuff, but also to push her wheelchair around and to take her places outside the Home."

"Yes, I'm sure I have seen this woman with your mother," Mrs. K said, "but I haven't met her. I assumed she was employed by the Home."

"No, she's not connected with the Home at all, although I believe she's married to the fellow who comes in to give massages. Or maybe she's his sister, I forget.

Same last name, anyway. And not only is she not paid by the Home, since Maria is with my mom several hours a day, the manager Mr. Pupik insisted mom pay an extra hundred dollars a month, just in case Maria sometimes ate lunch or dinner here or 'used the facilities,' as he put it."

"Or maybe used up some of the air or water?" Mrs. K said. She and Harold Pupik had never seen eye to eye on almost anything. That's because Pupik was a *momzer,* what you would call a bastard in less polite company. He ran the Home like a reform school, or maybe a prison, pinching pennies so hard Mr. Lincoln is choking, and treating the residents like inmates. But I suppose the board of directors liked how he saved them money and ran a "tight ship," as he liked to call it, because he had been here for many years.

"I know what you mean," Naomi said, "but mom had no choice and agreed to pay."

"I'll bet she wasn't very pleased about that," I said.

"That would be a huge understatement," Naomi said, smiling slightly. "I can't repeat what she calls him behind his back."

Mrs. K gave me a glance that expressed her feelings about this, but she said nothing further about it.

"Nevertheless, so far this all sounds quite positive," Mrs. K said in an encouraging voice. "Your mother has the help she needs, and fortunately she can afford it. About what is it you're so worried?"

"Yes, I was getting to that," Naomi said. She didn't look at all comfortable, still wringing the hands. "Maybe I'll take that tea you offered," she said to Mrs. K, who immediately got up and headed for the kitchen.

Looking back over her shoulder, she said, "Shall I

put a bit of *schnapps* in it, perhaps? You look like you could use it."

"Whiskey? No, no, I'm fine." Then, as Mrs. K turned back toward the kitchen, "Well, maybe just a drop." Clearly this was a serious business.

"Tea for you too, Ida?" Mrs. K asked.

"Yes, please," I said, "but no *schnapps*." I don't usually care for anything added to my tea, except sugar of course.

Mrs. K returned shortly with the tea and a small plate of *mandelbrot,* almond cookies. We munched and sipped for a minute or two, and then Naomi took a deep breath and continued her story.

"Well, like I said, mom hired this woman Maria. And at first she seemed to be the perfect companion: Cheerful, well-read and able to engage in intelligent conversations, strong enough to push or lift mom with no problem." Miriam Blumenthal was not a large woman and probably weighed no more than 100 pounds dripping wet, as they say.

Naomi paused to take a bite of cookie.

"And something happened to spoil all this perfection?" Mrs. K prompted. "Did Maria turn out to be a thief, stealing your mother's jewelry? Or a gossip, repeating confidential conversations?" Spreading gossip, called *lashon hara* in Hebrew, is a major sin in Jewish law.

Naomi shook her head. "No, nothing like that. It's hard to explain. Maria has sort of … well, sort of taken over mom's life."

Mrs. K and I looked at each other, puzzled.

"So what does this mean, 'taken over her life'?" I asked.

Naomi began wringing her hands again. "I mean, she tells mom what to do and not to do, what to buy, what to invest in … whom to listen to …."

A light suddenly went on in Mrs. K's eyes, as if she now understood.

"When you say 'whom to listen to,' is it Maria who she is saying to listen to, and perhaps you she is saying not to?"

Naomi looked up, now seeming more angry than worried. "Me and my brother, Barry. Yes, she's trying to cut us out of our mother's life. She tells mom all kinds of untrue things about us—she's a really good liar—as if we're just trying to get her money or something." Naomi's face was becoming quite pink.

"I see," Mrs. K said. "And of course there is a lot of money involved." Naomi nodded. "And is Maria telling your mother to give this money to her?"

"Not exactly. At least I hope not, although I can't really be sure. But she's convinced mom to buy certain investments without consulting us, investments that Barry and I think are real risky. And mom has been making some pretty large withdrawals from her bank account—I happened to see one of her bank statements when I visited her recently—and I don't know for what. Also, Maria's had her make an appointment with an attorney—Maria's attorney, not mom's—to see about making changes in her will."

"Ah. And do you know what are these changes?"

Naomi shook her head. "No, but I can imagine. Maria knows we don't like the way she's taken control of mom's life—Barry says he'd do anything to get rid of her—and I'm sure she wants mom to cut us out of her will, or worse yet, put her in!" Naomi's face was now quite red, and I thought she was about to *plotz*. Burst.

"Hmm. And what does your husband—Aaron, yes?—what does he say about all this?"

This seemed to agitate Naomi even more. "Aaron doesn't seem all that worried about it. In fact, he seems to be taking Maria's side! He keeps saying to keep out of mom's business and let her take care of herself. That Maria is a big help to mom and we should let her alone. You'd think he …"

But here she stopped, seeming even more upset than already she was. Apparently it was not a good idea to bring up Aaron in regard to this business. But who knew?

Mrs. K saw the same thing, and she tried to calm Naomi down.

"Naomi dear," she said in that soothing tone that is like your mother singing you a lullaby, "I'm sure it's not as bad as you fear. Miriam has always been a sensible lady, and it's hard to believe she would so easily be manipulated like you say."

Naomi didn't look convinced, but she said, "I hope you're right. In the past, mom has never let anyone take advantage of her. She could get pretty pissed off—oh, I'm sorry, I mean get really mad—if someone did. I remember she once threw an insurance salesman out of the house, literally, and down the front steps, when she thought he was trying to swindle her."

Naomi smiled as she said this. I myself had to smile at the thought.

"But that was a long time ago, when she was … was still okay, physically and mentally. Now I'm not so sure. I tried to warn mom about Maria, but she only said something like, 'I know exactly what I'm doing, and I can take care of myself,' and that was all she would

11

discuss it. But I think someone could easily take advantage of her …." Naomi's voice kind of trailed off, like she was thinking of that "someone." Then she looked up and said, "Anyway, the reason I wanted to speak to you was that maybe you could … could talk with mom and find out just what's going on. I've tried to ask, but that Maria has her so set against me and Barry …" Her voice trailed off again. Her eyes were now watering and she took a pretty flowered hanky from her pocket and dabbed at them.

Mrs. K and I looked at each other, then at Naomi, who looked so sad.

"Of course, Naomi dear," Mrs. K said. "We shall talk with Miriam and I'm sure we will find it's not as bad as you think. Mothers do not abandon their children so easily. But in any case, we shall see what we can find out and let you know."

Naomi sniffed once, put her hanky away, and stood up. She put her hand out to Mrs. K.

"Thank you," she said, looking at both of us. "I've been so upset about this, not knowing what to do. I hope you can get mom to tell you what that woman is saying to her."

"*Nu,* we shall see," Mrs. K said. "Meanwhile, try not to worry about it too much. In your mind such things can become exaggerated. Let's first find out what your mother has to say."

Naomi nodded. "I'll try." And she walked out, leaving Mrs. K and me to wonder whether this was a case of a well-meaning helper or an evil schemer. A *momzer* can be female as well as male.

Naomi's problem looked to be a simple one of a disagreement between family members and a person from the outside, a not uncommon thing. But one thing I've learned from my many adventures with Mrs. K is not to jump to conclusions. Things are not always as they appear. If Mrs. K is involved, you can be sure that what looks to be a sheep will probably turn out to be a goat.

Most likely a dead goat.

Chapter 3

Mrs. K and I decided to speak with Miriam
Blumenthal the following day. But the next morning, a
new development pushed its way to the top of our list.

We were finishing breakfast in the dining room,
sitting at our usual table. Sitting across from us, also as
usual, were our table companions, the always
distinguished-looking Isaac Taubman (with whom our
Mrs. K has been becoming quite intimate, if you know
what I mean) and Karen Friedlander (who I suspect
would like to become quite intimate with Taubman if she
had the chance).

Taubman asked nobody in particular, "So what do
you think they'll do for Purim this year?" Every year the
Home has some kind of Purim celebration, usually
involving children from one of the synagogues in town,
some of them the grandchildren of our residents. They
might dress up and put on a play, or recite from the
Megillah, which contains the story of Purim. Purim is
mostly a holiday for the children.

"I actually had an idea for something different,"
Mrs. K said. "I was going to run it by Pupik and see if
he'll go for it."

"Good luck with that," Taubman said. "I hope it
doesn't cost any money, because if it does, you can save
your breath. Remember when you asked Pupik to spend
a few dollars to fix up that empty room and buy a ping

14

pong table so we could get a little exercise when it was too cold to walk outside, and he acted as though it was a championship tennis court you had asked for?"

Mrs. K laughed. "Yes, I know. But in this case there is no extra cost."

"So what is this idea?" Karen asked.

"I thought perhaps we should turn the tables on the children this year. We will dress up and act out the story, and they will watch."

There was silence for a few moments. Then Taubman asked, "What do you mean 'we'? You and me and the other residents? Dress up like Queen Esther and Haman and Mordecai? Are you *meshugeh*?"

"Maybe it's crazy. It's just an idea. I haven't played Queen Esther since I was a little girl. Our *shul* would put on a Purim play every year. Once I even had to play Haman because we were short of boys. I didn't like that at all, playing such an evil person. Every time my name—I mean Haman's name—was mentioned, everyone spun their *groggers* at me." *Groggers* are noisemakers, shaped like an upside-down "L." The top part is metal and rotates against teeth in the handle and makes a very big noise. The idea is to drown out the name of the evil Haman, the Persian king's minister who wanted to exterminate all the Jews in Persia.

Sound familiar?

We all laughed at the thought of spinning *groggers* at respectable Mrs. K. She just smiled and rose from the table. "I agree it maybe sounds *meshugeh*," she said, "but perhaps that's just what would make it fun. Something to make us laugh at ourselves. Ida, let's go and ask Pupik what he thinks of the idea."

I myself didn't think much of it, and I doubted Pupik

would like it either. His sense of humor, if he had one, was a closely guarded secret; but of course I got up and accompanied my friend anyway. I couldn't let her approach Pupik by herself. It would be like letting her enter the lion's den without even a chair and a whip.

****

Pupik's office is in the administrative wing of the Home. Fortunately, on the way there we didn't again pass Moishe Klein, or anyone else, for that matter. Perhaps everyone was out in the garden on this sunny day. I wished I was too.

Pupik's office consisted of two rooms: An outer office where his secretary, Hilda, sits at a desk, and where there is also a round table for conferences, and an inner office, where the Supreme Ruler of the Home himself is found. Mrs. K knocked softly on the outer door, but there was no answer.

"That's right, I forgot that Hilda is away for a few days visiting her *mishpocheh*. I think her family is having some kind of celebration." Hilda Franklin, Pupik's secretary, we all admired for being able to work with a man like him, and at the same time pitied for having to do it; but she had been here for maybe ten years, so we assumed either she had an iron constitution, or she really needed the money.

Mrs. K opened the door and stepped in. Sure enough, no one was there. Hilda's desk was bare and her computer was covered. She is always so neat and orderly. When I was working, my typewriter didn't need a cover; it was never visible through the mess on top.

The room reflected Pupik's personality—colorless and strictly businesslike. Other than some bright objects and photographs of her children on Hilda's desk, it could as easily have been an office in a prison, or a funeral home. There were a few black and white photos of something, I think mountains, on the walls, and book shelves with a few books and a couple of shiny statues of some kind. On the shelves were only some newspapers and what looked like a shoebox. There was nothing else to brighten the place or make it welcoming. *Nu,* why should there be, as no one was welcome there.

"I'll go see if Pupik is in," Mrs. K said, and she walked over to the door to the inner office, which was at the other end of the room. I stayed by the outer door, perhaps feeling safer with an escape route nearby. When Pupik is in a bad mood, it's best to put as much distance between you and him as possible.

I stepped over to a bookshelf near me and looked more closely at one of the statues, which had a wood base underneath and on top was a man standing and aiming a gun—the short kind, like you see the bad guys and police detectives wearing inside their coats on TV. At the bottom was a shiny brass plate saying "First Place" was awarded to Pupik for "marksmanship." So it was some kind of trophy. I was surprised, not that he could shoot a gun straight or win a trophy, but that he apparently had a hobby other than making life difficult for the residents of the Home.

I also peeked inside the shoebox—I don't know why, it just seemed so out of place there with the trophies and other shiny things—and was surprised to see a small gun, a little like the one on the statue, but quite fancy, in an even fancier leather holder thing. With jewels on it yet. A funny place to keep a gun, but not my business. I closed the box and went back to the outer door.

Meanwhile, Mrs. K, who had stopped to examine

one of the photos on the wall, seemed to be about to knock on the inner office door, when her hand stopped in midair. On her face suddenly was a startled expression, as if her corset had just sprung apart, except I was pretty sure she was not wearing a corset. So at first I was puzzled, but then I realized there were voices coming from Pupik's office. There was some kind of argument going on in there, and the voices were leaking out through the frosted-glass door. I couldn't make out what was being said, but I assumed Mrs. K could, and whatever it was no doubt was responsible for the look of shock on her face.

Mrs. K seemed glued to the floor in front of the door for a minute or so, while she looked back at me with wide eyes. Then she turned and, making as little noise as possible, she hurried back to where I was standing. Mrs. K is a substantially built woman in her seventies, so to see her hurrying is not a pretty sight at the best of times. And this apparently was not the best of times.

When she reached me, she put her hand on my shoulder and turned me around toward the outer door, reached over to open it, and with her pushing me from behind, we made an undignified exit as if a crazed *dybbuk* were after us.

As it turned out, being chased by a demented ghost might have been preferable.

****

It was not until we had reached the safety of Mrs. K's apartment and caught our breath that I was able to learn what had so upset this woman who does not upset easily.

Naturally, before she could tell me, Mrs. K had to have a cup of tea to steady her nerves, and I needed one as well. So as soon as we were seated and sipping, I said, "*Nu,* so tell me already why we ran away, and from what. You looked like you had seen a ghost."

Mrs. K took a deep breath and said, "No, no ghost. And it isn't anything I saw; it is what I heard."

"Yes, I could hear voices too, but I couldn't tell what was being said."

"I heard very well as soon as I was in front of the door," Mrs. K said. "As you saw, I was about to knock, when I heard Pupik yelling."

"What was he saying?"

"He said something like, 'If you think you can just walk away like that, you're mistaken.' And then the other person, a woman, shouted something like 'Oh? Well just try to stop me.'"

"So who was this woman?"

"I couldn't tell. It was not familiar, the voice. I would say a younger woman, younger than Pupik, anyway."

"I see. *Nu,* so far it just sounds like an ordinary argument. Nothing to get so upset about, although of course you were right to leave …"

"No, no, Ida. You don't understand. I was upset by what was said after that."

"Which was?"

Mrs. K drank several sips of tea before answering. I was too absorbed in the story even to notice I was holding a cup. Finally she went on:

"The woman said, 'You got what you wanted, to get me into bed. All you wanted was a convenient mistress, someone you could … [and here Mrs. K stopped, apparently trying to find the right word] … someone you could *shtup,*' only she used the four-letter English word starting with 'F,' which I shall not."

I suddenly noticed that my mouth was hanging open, and I quickly closed it.

"Are you saying Pupik has been … has been *shtuping* someone behind his wife's back? An affair? A dumpy little *shmegegee* like him? *Oy vey!*"

"It takes all kinds, Ida. And he must have promised this woman something she considered worth the sacrifice. And whatever it was, it apparently was no longer sufficient to keep her … to keep her satisfied."

We were both silent for a minute. I was trying to absorb what was a most unpleasant picture, and then trying to un-absorb it as quickly as possible.

"So was there anything else?"

"I was so stunned, as you probably could tell, I couldn't immediately make my feet move. And just before I did, I heard Pupik shout, 'You'll live to regret this.' At that point I was afraid the door would open and Pupik and the woman would see I'd been listening and know their secret. It would not only be embarrassing for everyone, but it would make my past relationship with Pupik seem like a lovefest in comparison."

"No, it's not good to catch someone you know, even someone you don't like, with their pants down, so to speak. So is that all you heard?"

"That's all. It's more than enough, is it not?"

"Yes, much more," I said. "It's like stepping in a pile of dog *drek*: All you want to do is get it off your shoe as quickly as possible and hope the smell goes away."

But of course it was not that simple.

"So what do we do now?" I asked. "Anything? Or nothing? If Pupik is cheating on his wife, if he is going to bed with other women, can we just ignore it? Should it be reported to the Board of Directors? And does his wife not have a right to know?"

Mrs. K didn't answer right away. Finally she said, "I don't know, Ida. It's complicated. We both know it's a sin to spread gossip, even if it's true."

"But don't we owe some duty to Pupik's wife? Margaret is a nice person. We've always wondered why a person like her would marry a *momzer* like him, but I guess there's no accounting for taste."

"*Libe makht blind*, you know," said Mrs. K. "Love makes you blind."

"Yes, maybe," I replied, "but does it have to make you stupid? Anyway, can we let her be cheated on like this?"

"Well, Ida, for one thing, it looks like the cheating is over, at least for now. That woman, whoever she was, sounded pretty definite about it, although Pupik didn't seem to agree. Then there's the possibility that Margaret already knows, and there's no need for us to put our own ladle into the *borscht*. And for another thing, I don't believe every wife whose husband is cheating on them would even want to know. Sometimes, as they say, ignorance is bliss. Or at least it's less painful than knowledge."

"Not just for her," I said. "I would much prefer that we didn't know either."

I had nothing more to add. We both had to think this through.

I got up to leave, then sat down again. "You know, Rose," I said, "I think I will have some of that *schnaps* you offered to Naomi in my tea also."

I now needed it a lot more than did Naomi.

Chapter 4

The next day—it was now Wednesday—we had no time to worry about how, or whether, to deal with Pupik's shameful behavior. Purim was soon approaching and Mrs. K was determined to pursue her idea of the residents of the Home putting on a Purim play. I still thought it was a *meshugeh* idea, but I always trust Mrs. K when it comes to ideas: Hers are almost always better than mine. So I am giving her the benefit of the doubt here.

First, of course, we had to get Pupik's permission, something we had intended to do when we discovered his secret and had to make a fast retreat. So in the morning after breakfast Mrs. K and I again knocked on Pupik's office door. Again there was no response, Hilda still being away, and so again we opened the door and stepped into the outer office.

I have to admit I was more than a little nervous this time. Although it was quite unlikely we would encounter another "lover's quarrel" like the day before, somehow that remote prospect just added to the usual nervousness I feel when I'm around Pupik. It's not quite Daniel walking into the lion's den, but there is a definite similarity.

"I'll be honest, Ida," Mrs. K whispered as we closed the door behind us, "it's silly, but I'm not too anxious to go knock on the other door after what happened yesterday." So Mrs. K was feeling like I was, which was at least comforting. But she's not one to shy away from what has to be done, so she took a deep breath and almost marched to the door of Pupik's inner office and, after stopping to listen for any arguments that might be going on inside, knocked.

I heard Pupik shout, "Come in." Mrs. K, looking relieved, motioned for me to join her, and together we entered the lion's den. I mean office.

It's funny, but just knowing that Pupik was cheating on his wife changed the way I viewed the *momzer*. On the one hand, I liked him even less than I had before, for what he was doing and how it would affect his wife. On the other, I had to assume he must have some good quality to which this woman (not to mention his wife) was attracted. Maybe, as I've heard young people say in a similar situation, he was "good in bed."

Sure. And maybe the Pope had a bar mitzvah.

Once in the office, however, whatever new information I might have had, it appeared to be the same old Pupik. I could immediately tell from the look on his face that he was in one of his bad moods. Or maybe it's just one long bad mood, as he almost always seemed to be in it. At least he showed no signs of knowing that we knew what we knew. But whatever he was thinking, he asked us politely what we wanted.

Mrs. K cleared her throat and said, "I—we—would like to put on a Purim play."

"Yes, we have one here every year. The children put it on. What about it?"

"So this year, I—we—thought for a change we, that is, the residents, would put on the play and the families and the children would be the audience."

We waited for Pupik's reaction, which I assumed might be anything, from a simple "no" to a more elaborate rejection. But he just said, "Explain, please."

So Mrs. K proceeded to tell him her proposal in detail, that we would dress up in costume and use the props that the children usually use. I just nodded in agreement here and there, although I was not fully on board, as they say.

At first Pupik scowled and seemed not to like the idea at all. But then Mrs. K told him two things that clearly appealed to him.

"First, it will keep the residents occupied in a relatively harmless project for at least a week, making costumes and rehearsing the play." Pupik loved things that kept the residents occupied and out of his hair—what little hair he still had.

"And second, it will cost the Home almost nothing. Residents can make their own costumes, simple things like masks and crowns and three-cornered Haman's hats, out of heavy paper. We could even involve our grandchildren or local Sunday school classes in making some of the costumes. All the Home would have to contribute is a little money for supplies and refreshments. And we always pay for the refreshments even if the children put on the play as usual."

When Mrs. K had laid out the idea, Pupik said nothing, while he thought about it. At least I assumed he was thinking, as he had his arms folded and was staring down at his desktop. I hoped he would not take too long, as my feet were aching from standing there so long, and he had not asked us to sit down. Finally he looked up, put his hands on his desk, actually smiled a *bissel*, and said, "You know, ladies, I think you might have a good idea. Our residents are always asking for more and different activities, and this should shut … this should satisfy them on that score for a while." He then said something totally unexpected: "And I think the Home can pay for renting a costume or two."

The Home will pay? I had now heard everything.

We thanked him and made a hasty retreat before he could change his mind.

****

When we were back in the lounge and sipping tea, I asked Mrs. K, "Why do you think Pupik not only agreed to let us do this *meshugeh* play, which itself I had much trouble believing, but he said we could actually spend money on it? The Home's money? Which he treats as if it were his own?"

"Yes, I wonder too. And I can only speculate: Either he agrees with me that it is such a good idea it is worth risking a few dollars on it, or …"

"Or what? This would be maybe the first time, at least the first in my memory, he has agreed with you on anything. So what is the other possibility?"

"Or maybe he suspects that we know about his little affair. I don't know how he would, unless he somehow heard or saw us in his office yesterday, which I doubt; but it would certainly cause him to be, shall we say, more accommodating?"

I thought about this. Yes, if Pupik knew or suspected Mrs. K and I knew about him and his *tsaskela,* his plaything, that no doubt would make him most anxious to please us. I wondered for a moment what other "benefits" we might gain for the Home if that were the case, but I quickly dismissed the thought as unworthy. Delicious, but unworthy.

"Anyway," Mrs. K went on, "whatever the reason, we now have that little assignment to carry out. We shall order the necessary supplies, and go downtown to the costume shop tomorrow morning and rent the Purim paraphernalia."

****

In the morning after breakfast, I met Mrs. K in the lobby of the Home, ready to *schlep* downtown to pick out costumes. I had a feeling this idea of hers that we should put on the Purim play instead of the children would involve quite a bit of *schlepping* before it was over.

I didn't see the shuttle outside when I entered the lobby.

"Are we not going downtown this morning?" I asked Mrs. K when I saw her.

"Yes, we are. But it seems the shuttle is in the garage for repairs."

"So we'll be taking a taxi? Have you your senior discount card with you? Mine is in my room."

Mrs. K looked a bit uneasy. "Yes, I have mine," she said, "but we won't be using it."

"Surely we aren't going to walk," I said. "We might as well try to climb Mt. Everest. Or so my feet would tell you."

Mrs. K laughed. "No, no. We aren't walking."

"Nu, so what then? Fly?"

"I shall explain. I was asking Joy at the reception desk to call us a taxi when Sophie Glass taps me on the shoulder and says, 'If you're going downtown, Rose, why not come with me? While the shuttle is down, my grandson Sammy said I could drive one of his cars so I can get around.'"

"Her grandson has more than one car?"

"Apparently so. She said he has been a … what did she call him … a 'car nut' ever since he was a teenager, taking them apart and putting them together and 'souping them up' and all that, and now he still has several cars he likes to work on. The one he lent to Sophie must be one of his spares. Anyway, she said she was going downtown this morning and would love to have company. I guess I said we would be glad to ride with her."

I was a bit shocked. "I can't believe Sophie Glass still drives. *Gottenu!* She must be at least 85 years old and frail like a *faigeleh*. Like a little bird. And the glasses she wears are thick like hockey … hockey whatchamacallits."

"Pucks," said Mrs. K.

"I beg your pardon?"

"Pucks. Hockey pucks. Yes, they are quite thick, and she is delicate, as you say. I would not choose to ride with her, but … well, I didn't want to hurt her feelings by refusing. I couldn't very well say I—or we—didn't trust her driving, as we have never driven with her before. And I certainly couldn't say something like, 'I'm sorry, Sophie, but you're too old.'"

"No, of course not," I said. I sighed. There seemed to be nothing to be done except ride downtown with Sophie Glass.

****

A word here about Sophie. She was named after the great singer and actress Sophie Tucker—you knew Sophie Tucker was Jewish, yes?—who was a favorite of her mother at the time she born. I mentioned this to Mrs. K, not being sure she knew.

"Yes," she said, "Sophie told me. In fact, she said

27

she used to get very emotional whenever she heard a recording of *My Yiddishe Momme*, which of course was one of Sophie Tucker's most famous songs."

"Isn't that the song that Hitler banned because it was 'too Jewish'"?

"Yes—he was no better as a music critic than as a human being."

You shouldn't get the impression I had anything against Sophie as a person. She is a real *mensch,* a good and sweet person. But Sophie as a driver? I had my doubts.

****

Unfortunately, my doubts were more than confirmed when Sophie drove up in her grandson's car. I could see immediately why it was his "spare" car, as in "spare tire": it should only be used in case of emergency. My best guess is that this was Sammy's first car, and it was quite old when he bought it.

As soon as I saw the car, I grabbed Mrs. K's arm and said, "Rose, what is that Sophie is driving? It looks like it was used in the war and barely survived."

"Yes, Ida. World War One, most likely."

I will try to describe this machine. To say this car was big and old would be an understatement. The only time I have seen such cars before is in the movies, where *nogoodniks* like Albert Capone would sit in the back and smoke big cigars, unless they were being shot with machine guns, in which case the cars would end up looking like the colander I use to drain lentils. Its *tuchis* was up in the air and the front part down low, like it was one of those athletes in the Olympics getting ready to run a race. The body was painted black, although it had apparently been unpainted in several places. And *oy,* did it ever make a racket. And just to add frosting to the cake, it had bright red flames painted on the side, as if they were coming out of the motor. Maybe they were!

"I imagine," Mrs. K commented, "this was at one time quite an elegant automobile. Sophie's grandson probably didn't have the heart to send this car to the junkyard, so he kept it around so people like us would have the pleasure of riding in it." I don't think she was being serious. Such a pleasure we can easily do without, thank you.

I was the first to reach the car, which was making a low rumbling sound, I imagined something like a very large lion or tiger makes when getting ready to leap on an unsuspecting gazelle. I gingerly turned the handle of the rear door and pulled. Nothing happened. I pulled harder. Nothing happened. Finally Mrs. K grasped the handle with me and we both pulled. Even a growling tiger was no match for the combined weight of two determined ladies. The door swung open and it was all Mrs. K and I could do to keep from ending up head over *tuchis* in an undignified heap on the ground.

When we had finally climbed into the back seat, the car took off with a jerk and a roar.

That poor gazelle didn't have a chance!

The first thing we noticed when the car was moving was that we could not see anyone driving it. Looking over the high back of the front seat, we saw little Sophie peering over the top of the big steering wheel, the seat being pulled as far forward as possible so she could reach the pedals.

"Sophie," Mrs. K said, loud enough to be heard over the engine roar, "are you sure you can drive this … this vehicle?"

Sophie looked back, meaning she was not looking where the car was going, and said with a smile, "Oh, yes, Rose. Isn't it fun?"

If you define fun as having a heart attack, I suppose the answer was "yes."

"Sophie!" I called out. "Please watch where you're going."

"Oh, yes, sorry," she said, and turned around to face the front again, or as much of the front as she could see over the steering wheel.

There were no seatbelts in the back seat, and all we could do was hold onto each other's hands and pray this would not be our last ride. Just our last ride in this particular car.

I have ridden in many taxis, some of which it seemed were being driven by a *meshugener* bent on committing suicide. Sophie was neither crazy nor suicidal, but somehow I had felt much safer with the drivers who were.

Sophie actually managed to keep the car in the middle of the road—well, except for the one time she had trouble turning the wheel and scraped the paint off someone's garden fence—and to stop at all the red lights. When she stopped it was suddenly, and Mrs. K and I had to brace ourselves against the back of the front seat to avoid being launched through the front window like the stone with which David defeated Goliath.

Most fortunately, our prayers were answered and we arrived downtown in one piece, with the only damage being to our nerves. We climbed out of the beast as quickly as we could—Mrs. K had to swing her *tuchis* into the door to get it to open, not a pretty sight—and before Sophie could offer us a ride home later. We both thanked her effusively for delivering us, in more ways than one.

Sophie smiled and said, "You know, when my grandson loaned me this car, he said he wasn't sure I should be driving at my age. I told him people are too quick to equate old age with incompetence. It isn't a good idea to underestimate us seniors."

She gave us a wink, shifted gears with a crunching sound, stepped on the gas pedal, and the beast roared away, spitting smoke as it disappeared around the corner.

Who says young people have all the fun?

****

Before going to the costume shop, however, we made our way to the Garden Gate Café for a strong cup of tea.

For the second time in two days, I could have used a bit of *schnapps* with it!

Even without the added alcohol, however, the tea had the intended effect of settling our nerves.

When Mrs. K and I had finished our tea, I said to her, "So where to now, Rose? The costume shop?"

"Yes, I believe it's just a couple of blocks from here."

"And what sorts of costumes are we looking for? I doubt they will have much for Purim."

Mrs. K laughed. "There wouldn't be much demand, would there? But really, all we need are some generic king and queen costumes. The rest we'll have to make ourselves."

I hoped the "our" in "ourselves" was not intended to include me. I do not mind baking *hamantaschen*, to resemble Haman's hat. But I draw the line at making the hats themselves.

31

****

Perhaps at this point I should be telling you a little more in detail about the holiday Purim. It's not one of the "Big Three" Jewish holidays: Passover, Rosh Hashanah, and Yom Kippur. But it is one of the most fun to celebrate, especially for children.

The story of Purim is found in the Book of Esther, which we call the *Megillah*. (Now you know what it means "the whole *megillah*." The whole story.) Purim celebrates the time over two thousand years ago that Queen Esther saved the Jews of Persia from extinction. (You thought Hitler was the first one to try?)

When Queen Vashti disobeys the orders of Persian King Ahasuerus—he wanted she should come and show herself off to his friends, wearing only her crown, if you know what I mean—the king has her executed (who needed a divorce back then?) and holds a beauty contest to choose the next queen. *Nu,* when you are king, you can choose queens any way you want. The king falls in love with Esther, a beautiful young Jewish woman, although he doesn't know she is Jewish, and selects her to be queen.

Meanwhile, Haman, the king's wicked prime minister, has convinced the king to have all the Jews in the kingdom killed, in part because Mordecai, Esther's cousin and a leader of the Jewish community, had refused to bow down to him. He has even had the gallows built to hang Mordecai. Mordecai learns of this plan and tells Esther, who goes to the king and asks him to hold a gala ball. At the ball, she tells the king not only is she Jewish, but Haman is planning to kill all of her people. The king, obviously preferring Esther to Haman, has Haman hung on the gallows instead of Mordecai, who he appoints prime minister. The Jews celebrate. And now you know why we spin the *groggers* and make noise to drown out Haman's name whenever it is read in the *Megillah*.

The story is a lot more complicated than this, of course, but you get the idea. It's another case of "They tried to kill us, they failed, let's eat." In this case, what we eat a lot of is *hamantaschen,* the little three-cornered pillows of dough that I mentioned earlier, and which are filled with jam or prunes or poppy seeds. Also a special sweet *challah* and dishes made from beans (apparently Esther was a vegetarian). The *hamantaschen* represent Haman's three-cornered hat. Some people say they represent Haman's ears, but I prefer not to think I'm eating someone's ears, even Haman's. I don't know if the expression "eat your hat" comes from this, but it is one hat of which you should definitely take a *nosh.*

****

The shop Mrs. K took us to was called "The Costume Party," and it was like walking into the middle of that thing they hold every year in New Orleans. Masks, balloons, streamers everywhere.

There was no one around, so Mrs. K tinkled the little bell with a button on top that is sitting on the counter. Still no one, so Mrs. K gives the bell such a good *patsh* that it slid right off the counter and onto the floor, where it bounced a few times, making its ringing sound every time it landed. This apparently was enough to get the clerk's attention, because he came rushing out from somewhere in back to see what was the trouble.

When he saw us standing there, he gave us a not-so-friendly look. He bent down to pick up the bell where it had come to the end of its little excursion and placed it back on the counter. He then gave us a painted-on smile like he had borrowed it from one of his masks.

"Yes, ladies? Can I help you?"

"We are looking for Purim costumes. For a play."

He did not blink, as if people came in every day requesting Purim costumes. Maybe they did.

"What did you have in mind? We have kings, queens, Haman, the usual."

Usual? Purim must be very popular around here. We learned later that because this is the only costume shop in town, and all the synagogues in the area put on some kind of Purim play every year, they all rent their Purim costumes here. We ended up renting one king, two queens, and several Haman masks. Also we bought several dozen *groggers* to make noise during the reading of the *Megillah*. They would be delivered a few days before Purim.

****

Mrs. K made an announcement at dinner about the Purim play and asked for volunteers to take the parts and also to help with decorations and such. She also urged everyone to come to the play, invite the family (especially children), and everyone should wear a costume or at least a mask to make it a really festive occasion. It seemed most of the residents liked the idea, and there was a real buzz of conversation following the announcement.

Perhaps this wasn't such a *meshugeh* idea after all.

The next day, Mrs. K and I spoke with Rabbi Rosen, from the local Conservative synagogue, who officiates at any services held at the Home. We asked him if we could borrow the script for the Purim play. Each year the children in their Sunday school put on the play at their synagogue and then they come to the Home and perform it again for us. We explained that this year, they would be invited to come and watch us perform the play for them.

Rabbi Rosen seemed to think this would be a nice change and not only agreed to lend us the script, but he offered to lend us some of the props they use.

Everything was ready for the big production.

Next stop, Broadway?

Chapter 6

After lunch, Mrs. K and I decided to speak with Miriam Blumenthal, as we had promised to do. We hadn't seen her at her usual table, so we made our way to her apartment.

Mrs. K knocked on Miriam's door, but there was no answer. We were about to leave when Naomi approached us and called out.

"Mrs. Kaplan, wait. I wanted to talk to you."

We waited. Naomi hurried up to us, panting a bit from the exertion. (It wouldn't hurt her to lose a few pounds.)

"We wanted to speak with your mother," Mrs. K said, "but she doesn't seem to be home."

"Yes, that's exactly what I wanted to talk to you—to you both—about."

"That she's not home? So where is she?"

"That's just the problem," Naomi said. "I don't know. But I found out that lately Maria has been taking her out several times a week. Mother says they're just going to the park or to a movie, but I don't think she's telling the truth. It's been too cold for the park lately, and the other day, when she said they went to the movies, she couldn't tell me anything about the story."

It happens to me all the time, not being able to remember a movie's plot the next day after seeing it, but I didn't say anything.

"Hmm. So where do you think they're going?" Mrs. K asked.

"I suspect Maria's been taking her to see her—that is Maria's—lawyer, or maybe her stock broker or something. It's all part of a plot to get her money, I just know it." Naomi was again getting quite emotional.

Mrs. K put a hand on Naomi's arm. "Now you may be getting upset over nothing. People do go to the park in cold weather, and at her age, your mother has every right to forget the movie she just saw."

Naomi shook her head slowly. "Maybe you're right, but I'd feel much better knowing where she goes."

"Yes, I suppose so," Mrs. K said. "So when we do get a chance to speak with your mother—and I'm sure it will be soon—we will be sure to ask her about this."

"You won't tell her I wanted to know, will you?" Naomi asked.

Mrs. K smiled and patted Naomi's hands, which the poor girl was wringing like the wet wash. "Don't worry. I will ask her diplomatically, of course."

Naomi was still looking most uncomfortable, staring at the floor. "I guess I was thinking that maybe you could, you know, follow her or something."

"Follow her?" I said.

Naomi nodded her head. "I would follow her myself one of these afternoons, but I don't drive, and a taxi … well, it's not like in the movies where you can just tell the taxi driver to 'follow that car,' is it?"

We both agreed it was not.

"And I'm afraid if she sees me following her, it will just cause more trouble between us …"

"Naomi dear, neither Ida nor I drives, at least any more, and even if we did …"

"Maybe you could get someone to drive you," Naomi almost pleaded. She had obviously become obsessed with this idea of finding out where Maria takes her mother.

It was at this very point that one of us—preferably Mrs. K—should have said quite clearly to Naomi, "No, we have no intention of playing private detective and secretly following your mother, like in the movies. If you want her followed, do it yourself." That is what one of us should have said.

Unfortunately, neither of us said that. Instead, we hesitated just long enough to give Naomi the impression we were actually considering it. From there it was all downhill to "Well, I don't know …" followed by "I guess we might …" and before we knew it, one of us—I am honestly not sure who—had said we would "see what we could do."

Oy vey.

****

Back in my apartment, I asked Mrs. K the obvious question: "Just how are we supposed to find out where Miriam is going? We don't drive, and we certainly are not going to ask Sophie to take us in that death trap she's driving."

Mrs. K laughed. "No, Ida, and not only because it's not safe. Can you imagine trying to 'tail' someone, as they call it in the movies, without them knowing, in a car that makes such a racket and looks so strange? We might as well announce over a loudspeaker, 'Look behind you, Miriam, and see who is following you.'"

"So in what do we follow her? A bus?"

"No, Ida, but I have a suggestion. We have in the past imposed upon your niece Sara to drive us places. Do you think she might be willing to help us follow Miriam?"

To be honest, I had not thought of asking Sara, but Mrs. K's suggestion was a reasonable one. Sara, who is retired from her job as a legal secretary and living on her well-invested inheritance, has always enjoyed an adventure, and in the past she has done more than just drive us places. She and her friend Florence, the lady burglar (but that is another story), have helped Mrs. K and me—well, mostly Mrs. K—to solve more than one mystery here at the Home.

Yes, it was a good idea, except for one small thing.

"With Sara I have no problem," I said. "But if you remember, she drives that big blue monster car—what was it, her father's old Buick? We would be as noticeable following Miriam in that car as in Sophie's."

"Hmm. You're right. So maybe she has a new car by now? It can't hurt to ask."

I told Mrs. K I would telephone Sara right away.

****

"Auntie Ida! How are you? It's been a while since I heard from you. How is Mrs. Kaplan? Has she solved any more murders lately?"

Oy, so many questions in one breath, and all I had said was "Hello, Sara?"

"Sara, dear. Yes, it has been a little while since we talked. And it seems every time I telephone you, I'm asking a favor. But this time it has nothing to do with a murder. No one has died, even." I explained about Naomi and her mother.

"So you want me to drive you around as you tail this woman Miriam and her … her evil companion?" She was laughing as she said it.

"Yes, although it sounds a bit silly when you say it like that."

"I suppose so, but you and Mrs. Kaplan do get up to some pretty bizarre adventures. Like the time she climbed through that window …"

"Yes, yes, I know, dear. But this is much different. Like I said, there is no murder. Just a worried daughter."

"Okay. And you know I'm always ready to help you out. I suppose I can drive the getaway car this time."

"What getaway? It's Miriam who is getting away. We're just following her. Anyway, I appreciate that you're willing to help. There's only one thing that's a problem."

"What's that?"

"It's your car. I mean, it isn't exactly blending in with all the others. And if we are not to be noticed …"

Again Sara laughed. "Yes, I see what you mean. My dear old Buick. Hmm … let me think."

She thought. I waited. After a minute, she finished thinking.

"I'll tell you what," she said. "I'll ask my boyfriend if we can borrow his car. He drives a real plain-vanilla something sedan. I think it's a Honda, but it could be a Ford or a Toyota. They all look alike to me these days. That's why I like my old Buick."

"Do you think he will let you borrow it?" I asked.

"Oh, sure. We're in that early part of our relationship where he's still trying to get me into bed with him. He won't want to louse it up."

I didn't know exactly how to respond to this. I think it was what my granddaughter likes to call "too much information."

When I didn't say anything, Sara said, "Auntie Ida?

Are you still there?"

"Yes, dear. I guess I lost my train of thought. Please let me know after you've spoken with your young man. About borrowing his car, I mean."

"What else would I … ? Oh, I see." She laughed. "Did I tell you more than you needed to know? Sorry— I was just kidding. I'll ask him and call you back."

"That will be fine, dear.

"And take my advice: Don't ask him while you're in bed."

Chapter 7

The next day Sara phoned to say her friend Tom—her "current significant other," as she put it—had agreed to lend her his car. They had planned an outing, as she put it, that day, but she explained to him that she was needed here, as was his car.

"That's very nice of him," I said, "and of you, dear."

"So when will you want me to chauffeur you in your little tailing job?"

"Tailing? Oh, I see what you mean. I don't know, because I don't know exactly when Miriam will be leaving with Maria. It's usually about three in the afternoon."

"Every day?"

"Almost, from what Naomi says. So will it be alright if you come here tomorrow at, say, two-thirty in the afternoon, and if we see Miriam leaving, we'll follow."

"And if not?"

"If not, *nu,* then you'll have to come back the next day. I'm sure it won't be more than two days you will have to come."

Sara laughed. "Don't worry, Auntie Ida. I love visiting with you and Mrs. Kaplan. Even if it takes three times, that's okay."

A real *mensch,* is Sara. And that is how we left it.

****

As it turned out, Sara only had to come one day,

because the day after we spoke, promptly at three in the afternoon, Maria pushed Miriam's wheelchair out to her, that is, Maria's, car, which was in the employee parking area a little farther away than where visitors park. Sara, Mrs. K, and I had been sitting in the lobby waiting to see if they left, and as soon as they went out the front door, we sprang up—no, to be accurate, Sara sprang up; Mrs. K and I just stood up, as our springs have long since rusted—and walked out to Sara's car. She had parked right out in front in the passenger loading area. (It isn't kosher, but no one complained.) It was a not-so-new silver Honda Civic, or so the badge on its back side said, which looked like a thousand other cars on the street, perfect for snooping. I got in next to Sara, and Mrs. K climbed into the back seat.

By the time Maria's car—it was plain white, but I have no idea what kind of car it was—was leaving the Home's parking lot, we were able to fall in line behind it.

"According to Naomi, Miriam says they usually go to the park or a movie, so unless Naomi's suspicions are correct, I assume that is where we're headed," Mrs. K said to Sara.

"If it's to the park, they're going the wrong way," Sara said, turning around to speak to Mrs. K. I do wish she wouldn't do that on a busy street.

"Yes, I see that," Mrs. K said. "So it's either the movie theater or …"

But just then the white car made a sharp turn onto a freeway ramp. Sara had to swerve to follow them, sending us sideways as far as the car's seatbelts let us slide.

"I guess they're not going to the movies, either,"

Sara said.

Not unless the movie was playing in a neighboring city.

****

We were now driving on a highway. Sara was staying a few cars back of Miriam and Maria, just like they do it on TV. I was beginning to feel like I was in the middle of one of those TV detective stories. But why not, with Mrs. K sitting behind me? Looking back, the adventures I have had with her would fit very nicely on cable television.

As we drove, Sara turned to me and said, "By the way, Auntie Ida, did you know Uncle Max is coming for a visit?"

This certainly got my attention. I hadn't been in touch with my brother Max in quite a while. I don't know why, as we always got along well. He lives somewhere in Alaska, or at least he did the last time I heard from him. Not a place I am likely to visit soon.

"So your mother has been corresponding with Max?"

"Yes, they've written to each other a few times a year, I'd say. Mom invited him to visit, and he said he'd be here next week. I'm anxious to see him. I think the last time was when I had my bat mitzvah, and you know how long ago that was!"

"That is a long time," I said. "I think I last saw Max when his wife passed away and we all gathered for the funeral and the *shiva* service. I hope I'll have a chance to see him while he's here."

"Oh, I'm sure mother will invite you over when he's here. In fact, I believe he specifically asked mother to do that. It's a big deal seeing him after all this time."

I turned around and said, "Rose, I guess you've never met my brother Max?"

"No," she said, "but you have mentioned him to me, and I'd like to meet him when he visits. But isn't he the one you said the family calls "Weird Uncle Max"?

Sara and I both laughed at this, because it was true. Max was always what you might call "eccentric," at least to be polite about it. Nothing serious, just that he was always clowning around, playing practical jokes, that kind of thing. We never knew what Max would do next.

"Max is six years older than me," I said. "He was always the joker in the family, with his practical jokes and silly *meshugass*."

"So he was hard to live with?" Mrs. K asked.

"At times yes, but he was the kind of boy it was hard to be mad at. I mean, he didn't mean any harm, he was just having fun."

"And did he outgrow the *meshugass*?"

"No, not really. Of course, his tricks and jokes changed as he got older, but to this day he likes to have his fun, tell jokes, sometimes not so respectable ones."

"Is he this way all the time?"

"Actually, he can be quite serious at times, though rarely in public. He's really extremely intelligent—graduated very high in his class at university and had a successful career as a … I think a biologist is what you call it. Anyway, when he's not joking around and is talking to you in his serious mood, he's very interesting to listen to. But most people don't get to see that side of him. They probably think he's just a joker and not very smart.

"You know, we really don't know all about a person unless we actually live with them, and even then there can be sides of their personality that are hidden from us."

"That's true," Mrs. K said. "How many times have we read about someone who did some terrible thing, like commit murder, and all of his friends and even family say they can't believe it, he was always such a gentle, peaceful person. Never hurt a fly. But it's not that this person changed overnight; it's more likely there was a side of him they hadn't seen."

"Maybe that's so," Sara said, "but I assure you that in Max's case, he's not dangerous, just a little strange. But I assume he's mellowed a lot by now. At least I hope so." She turned to me. "Remember that time he put the red pepper in the *borscht* …"

"Yes, yes. But that was a long time ago. I'm sure he behaves himself now." To myself, I added, "At least I hope so."

With all this talk, Sara almost missed seeing the white car we were following turn off the highway. She did the same.

"Where do you suppose this is leading us?" Mrs. K asked.

"As far as I know," Sara replied, "the only thing out here is the Red Feather casino. It's run by the local Indian tribe. But surely they couldn't be going there."

Maybe they couldn't, but they were, just the same. Because the white car turned right after leaving the highway and then into a wide driveway. Over the driveway was a sign big enough to see several miles away. It said, "Red Feather Casino" and "Entrance," and it was filled with blinking red lights in the shape of a feather. Understated it was not.

"Maybe they're just looking for a place to eat," Sara said.

"Or a restroom," I added. I could have used one myself.

Mrs. K didn't sound convinced. "Hmm. Maybe. I wonder ..."

The white car parked, and we then parked several spaces away. We watched as Maria got Miriam's folding wheelchair out of the trunk, opened it up, and helped Miriam out of the car and into the wheelchair. When they were walking to the casino entrance, we got out of our car and followed.

Even more than before, I felt like I was in a television story.

It was a *bissel* exciting.

Chapter 8

I should mention that I had never been in a casino until that day. It's not that I don't approve of what goes on there, the gambling and such. Well, maybe I don't. But it's also that people I know who have been there tell me it's crowded, smoky, and very noisy. If I want crowded, smoky, and noisy, and without the gambling, I can go to the "Tick Tock Tavern" that I sometimes pass when I'm walking near the Home. The noise and smoke are leaking onto the sidewalk, and I walk faster to get past it.

So this was quite an education for me. As soon as we were through the big front doors, keeping the ladies in sight, I found that my friends were right. *Oy,* the *tumel*! If I had known, I would have brought ear plugs and a gas mask. My eyes were already watering from the smoke, and it smelled like the inside of an ashtray, not that I've ever been inside an ashtray but if I were, I am sure this is how it would smell.

Apart from the noise and the smell, the inside of the casino looked like the pictures I have seen of Las Vegas, the part they call the Strip. Everywhere there were neon signs and blinking lights, sometimes chasing themselves from one side of the wall to the other and back. What with all the lights and the sounds, it was hard to think, much less talk.

"If this is where Maria and Miriam are choosing to

eat," I almost shouted to Mrs. K, "I hope they never invite me to dinner."

But they did not head for the restaurant, or the restroom for that matter. They went into the big room where most of the noise was coming from and where hundreds of people were standing or sitting in front of what I assumed were slot machines. The people looked like mechanical dolls, moving only their arms, first to put something into the slot on top, then pulling down a handle on the side. The machines then made doodly-doodly sounds and pictures spun around in a little window, while lights on the machines blinked in different colors and patterns. Sometimes a little ticket thing came out, but mostly the people just put more money in the slot and pulled the handle again.

"They don't look very happy," I said to Sara. I again had to almost shout to be heard.

"No, they don't, do they?" she said. "More like they're hard at work. I guess the only time they smile is when they win something."

And just then something else happened that almost made me *pish* in my pants, you'll pardon the expression. Right next to me the machine seemed to explode, with loud bells and more doodly-doodly sounds, only ten times louder than before. The woman standing in front of the machine started shouting and jumping up and down like she had a bad case of *shpilkes*, pins and needles.

I put my hands over my ears, as did Mrs. K over hers. Sara just laughed and pulled us away from the machine. "They sure get excited when they get a jackpot," she said. Of course, I knew what a jackpot was, but I had never associated it with the craziness I was now looking at.

So I guess this is what all those people without smiles pulling those handles were waiting for. From the look of it, most of them had been waiting a very long time.

We were following Sara, who was keeping Miriam and Maria in sight. Which is a good thing, because I could not see them in all the smoke and crowd. Suddenly Sara stopped next to a bank of machines that said "5 cents," put her arm out, and said, "Wait. They've just stopped in front of that slot machine over there. Let's see what they do."

I hoped it would not take long, because I could not take much more of the smoke and *tumult* inside that building.

It did not. It was now clear why Maria had brought Miriam to this casino. They were in front of a machine with flashing lights over it that said "$1." It appeared to be specially made so someone in a wheelchair could put in the money and pull the handle. It should not be said these people do not cater to the disabled.

What happened next I found hard to believe. Miriam took out of her purse what looked like a credit card and gave it to Maria. Maria then went to a little booth at the center of the room and came back with some kind of tokens, like I saw other people around us had, and handed them to Miriam. And then Miriam put them into that machine and began pulling the handle as fast as she could. The look on her face was just like that on most of the other faces in that room.

It was obvious she too was looking for a jackpot. And with the same grim determination.

****

We watched for a few more minutes, and then Sara turned to us and said, "I think we've pretty well seen what there is to see. Who knows how long they might be here, and I've got to get Tom's car back pretty soon."

"That's fine, dear," Mrs. K said. "I think we know now where Maria takes Miriam, at least when it isn't to the park or the movies." She turned to me and said, "Shall we go, Ida?"

I'm afraid I didn't answer her right away. While we were waiting and watching, my feet hurt so bad I had sat down on a stool in front of one of the "5 cent" machines. (I later learned these were a few old-fashioned machines from the days when people put coins into them and if they won, more coins came out the bottom, instead of little tickets like now.) I noticed there were two nickels someone had left in the little tray at the bottom of the machine.

I honestly do not know why I did what I did next, but I picked up one of the nickels and put it into the slot at the top of the machine. I pulled on the handle at the side, like I saw everyone else doing. What happened next nearly made me *plotz*! These colored wheels in a little window spun around and around and when they stopped, three pieces of fruit were showing in the windows. I think one was an orange, also some cherries. Maybe ten nickels fell into the little tray to join the one I had left there! Suddenly I wanted to see if I could make that happen again. I might even win a jackpot and thousands of nickels will pour out of the machine and lights will flash and ….

I picked up one of the nickels from the tray and put it in the slot and pulled the handle again.

Nothing happened, of course, and just as I was about

to do the same with the next nickel, I turned around and saw Mrs. K and Sara staring at me. I felt as if I'd been caught with my hand in the cookie jar. And at my age!

Suddenly Sara burst out laughing. "Auntie Ida, I didn't know you were a gambler. Maybe I shouldn't have brought you here. I hate to interrupt you when you're winning," she said looking at the tray with the nickels in it, "but we have to go."

I started to explain that I wasn't gambling and had just sat down for a rest, but neither Sara nor Mrs. K looked like they believed me.

"You know," Mrs. K said to Sara, "I think this gambling habit is contagious. Already Ida has caught it. We should leave before we're all standing in front of those machines losing our money."

Mrs. K took me by the arm and helped me up.

"But don't forget your winnings, Ida," she said, scooping out the remaining nickels from the tray. "Gambling may be a bad habit, but a nickel is still a nickel."

And so did my gambling career both begin and end in a five-minute period.

From now on, I decided, a game of dreidel with my grandchildren at Chanukah will be my only vice.

****

We made our way out of the Red Feather Casino, and *oy,* was I glad to breathe the fresh air again. And to be out of the noise. We didn't have to shout at each other to be heard.

As we drove back on the highway, we discussed what we had seen.

"It's possible," I said, "that this is the only time Maria has taken Miriam to that place. Anyone might go there just to see what it's like."

"Yes, it's possible," Mrs. K said, "but personally I don't think it is the first time, or the last. You saw how they went straight for the special machines for the handicapped. And how Maria immediately got a card from Miriam and knew just where to take it. And how grimly determined Miriam looked. It all seemed to me like a familiar routine."

"I have to agree with Mrs. Kaplan, Auntie Ida," Sara said. "They did seem to know the drill pretty well."

"Yes," I said to Mrs. K, "now that you point it out, I agree too. But what does that mean regarding what Naomi wants to know? Is it important that her mother gambles at a smoky casino?"

"That depends," Mrs. K said. "I suppose Naomi will be glad Maria was not taking her mother to see a lawyer or a banker. But this might be even more of a worry. If Maria is helping Miriam to gamble, and if Miriam is losing a lot of money in those machines, that cannot be a good thing."

"No," Sara said. "I've known people who've had a gambling habit, and it can ruin you. I used to go out with this one guy who would occasionally go to the race track and bet a few dollars there. He even took me along once, and it was fun. I think I lost four dollars myself. But then I started to notice that he never seemed to have any money, always asking me to pay for things when we went out because he was 'a little short' that week or 'had some big expenses come up.' Turned out he'd started going to the track several times a week and betting more and more money—I should say losing more and more money—and even borrowing from other people just to get along. Had a good job and everything, but ended up broke."

"I assume you stopped seeing the *schlemiel*," I said.

"I did, but actually I felt sorry for him. It was like a disease he couldn't control. He was more a sick person than a bad one."

We were all quiet for a few minutes, as we thought about Miriam and what this all meant. Finally, Mrs. K said, "Of course, we don't know that Miriam has anything like such a sickness as Sara's friend. We could be mistaken, and this may actually be the first time Maria has taken her there." She didn't sound like she believed it, though.

"So are you going to tell the daughter where her mother was taken?" Sara asked.

After a pause to think, Mrs. K said, "I'm not sure, Sara. On the one hand, we only followed Miriam because Naomi wanted to know where she went. But on the other hand, Naomi was mostly concerned that Maria was taking her to see a lawyer, or something like that. Telling her that her mother went to a casino might only cause trouble. It's something we'll have to think about.

"One thing is for certain, though: Maria is not doing Miriam any favors taking her to such a place. It is at least bad judgment, and worse if going there was Maria's idea.

"I'd say Naomi has good reason to be worried about her mother in that woman's care."

Chapter 8

While we were driving back to the Home, Sara changed the subject from Maria and Miriam to me.

She asked, "Why don't you learn to drive yourself, Auntie Ida? I see lots of people your age, and even older, driving."

I immediately thought of our recent ride with Sophie Glass in the gangster car. Yes, people older than me drive.

I could understand Sara asking. This was not the first time I had had to call on her for transportation. And although she has always been very sweet about it, I could tell she was not happy being called away from an important engagement—*oy,* I wish an engagement was what it really was, such a waste that she's not married— to drive me around. So I wasn't so surprised when she suggested that I learn to drive.

Again.

"Sara dear, you are probably too young to remember, but once before I learned to drive. Or rather I should say I took the lessons. Learn I did not."

"I didn't know that," Sara said. "Who did you take lessons from?"

"It was from one of those companies that advertise in the newspaper that they will teach you to drive in only two days. Or maybe it was two weeks. It could have been two years and it wouldn't have made a difference."

"What happened? Did you have an accident? Wreck the car or something?"

"No, no. Nothing like that. Although I'm sure poor Mr. Pomerantz—I still remember his name—wished I had smashed into something right at the beginning, so he would have missed what came after."

"Was he a poor teacher?"

"No, just unlucky. To get me as a student, I mean."

"So tell me what happened already. Obviously it was a traumatic experience."

"From trauma I don't know, but it was certainly an experience."

"When was this?"

"Not recent. It was just after your uncle David, of blessed memory, had passed away. He had always done the driving for us, so a license I had no need for. But when he was gone and I was living alone—this was before I moved to the Home and was still in our old house—I either had to take the bus or a taxi, or beg a ride from a neighbor. *Nu,* as I have been begging rides from you."

"So you decided to learn to drive yourself?"

"I did. I telephoned to the A-1 Driving School. It was the first one listed in the phone book. The next day I took my first lesson."

"And how did it go?"

"It went. The instructor Mr. Pomerantz was a nice young man, who greeted me with a big smile on his face. He obviously thought it was going to be a pleasant experience teaching me to drive. The poor unlucky *schlemazl,* he didn't know what he was getting himself into."

"That bad, huh?"

"You should have seen it. First he pointed out all the levers and gadgets and showed me how they worked. I should have taken notes. I had driven a car as a girl, but this one was very different. Then he asked me to start the motor. I did, but I forgot to let go of the key after I turned it. *Oy,* what a racket that made. But apparently the motor survived and was running. So next he told me to put the car in gear."

"Was it an automatic transmission?"

"No, I had to pull on this big lever until a letter D appeared in a little window."

"Yes, that's what they call automatic."

"Whatever. Finally I got started, and we drove around a big empty parking lot a few times until I was more familiar with all the gadgets. After a little while doing that, he said we should go out on the street."

"And how did that go?"

"*Nu,* things were going along very nicely, thank you, until the problem with Second."

"You mean getting into second gear? If it was automatic …"

"No, I mean Second Avenue, where the traffic light changed from green to red just as we were almost there."

"Oh, dear. Did you stop?"

"Did I stop? Of course I stopped. Immediately. But the *shmegegi* behind me did not stop. At least not until the front of his car met the back of our car."

"Geez, was anyone hurt?"

"No, fortunately neither car was going very fast. Only our bumpers met and exchanged greetings. A light tap."

"No harm, no foul, I guess."

"What?"

"Nothing. So what did your instructor say?"

"Poor Mr. Pomerantz, he was not doing well at all."

"I thought you said no one got hurt in the accident."

"Not so much hurt. It was his nerves. He must have been a very nervous person, because even though I stopped the car well before the middle of Second Avenue, and like I said his automobile was not damaged at all, his face was pale and he looked like he would have liked to get out and take a bus back to his office."

Sara laughed. "But I assume he stuck with it."

"He had a choice? We couldn't just leave the car there."

"I guess not. So did the rest of the lesson go better?"

"It did, *danken Got.* That is, we made it back to the office without hitting anything. We did just miss a school bus and a gentleman in a crosswalk—I've never seen an old man move so fast—but we made it. When we stopped in front of the office, you should have seen the look of relief on poor Pomerantz's face. I'm sure he *pished* his pants before we got there."

"I'll bet. So then you do know how to drive."

"Yes and no. I know about the levers and the gadgets and how to steer and all that, but driving on the street is another matter entirely. No, I decided if God had wanted me to drive, He would have given me wheels. I leave all the driving to others like you, even if I am sorry to put you to so much trouble."

"It's no trouble, Auntie Ida. I just thought it would be more convenient for you if you didn't have to rely on other people to go places."

"Listen, Sara, there are not so many places I go these days, and usually I take a taxi or the Home's shuttle. It's hardly ever I have to ask for a ride. So I hope you don't mind if on occasion I do."

Sara patted my hand and said, "Not at all. In fact, it was kind of exciting following those women today. Like in a real detective story. In fact, it seems whenever I get mixed up with you and Mrs. Kaplan together, there's some kind of mystery involved. So count me in."

"Thank you, Sara dear. We both appreciate it. And as a little reward, I have some delicious *hamantaschen* I baked getting ready for Purim. Come in and *fress.*"

"Sounds good. All this detective stuff works up an appetite."

Chapter 9

With all of the talking about this Maria and the following her and everything, we had still never actually met her. To us, she was still a stranger. This changed, however, the very next day. We were walking down the hallway on our way to breakfast when we passed Miriam Blumenthal's door. Miriam was just then coming out of her room, being pushed in her wheelchair by Maria.

Naturally, we stopped to say good morning, and Miriam said, "Have you two met Maria Cartwright, my new helper? She's married to John Cartwright, you know, the man who comes here twice a week to give us massages."

Mrs. K said, "Of course, we have seen you with your companion together many times, but we haven't actually had a chance to meet her."

She turned to Maria, put her hand out, and said, "I'm very pleased to meet you, Mrs. Cartwright. It's such a *mitzvah* to help another person like you do."

I was not so sure it was a *mitzvah* (which means "commandment," but in this context is a "good deed") when Maria was getting well paid to do it, but I guess Mrs. K was just being polite.

"Likewise," I added.

Maria smiled like an angel and shook both our hands. In fact, she looked a little like an angel. A real *shainkeit,* a beautiful young woman. Blonde hair, blue eyes, and the shape like one of those bathing suit models—the kind of face and figure women wish they had, and men wish they could get.

"It's nice to meet you both," she said. "And please, call me Maria. Miriam has mentioned you both, and especially you, Mrs. Kaplan. I understand you've actually solved a mystery or two here at the Home."

I expected Mrs. K to respond with some modest comment about how she only tried to help the police a *bissel*, as she usually does when someone brings up her detecting. But she did not. In fact, it seemed like she caught her breath, as if she had just had a sharp pain or something. Then after a few seconds she managed to say in a weak voice, "We won't keep you. I hope we have a chance to get better acquainted." It was as if it was an effort just to speak.

We stood there as Maria, still smiling, pushed Miriam's wheelchair down the hall in the direction of the dining room. It was the direction in which we had been headed, only now Mrs. K, who looked pale as a sheet, as my mother would say, walked slowly over to a bench at the side of the hallway and sat down.

I was scared there was something terribly wrong with her. After all, even strong, healthy people, like Mrs. K had always been, when they get to our age, can suddenly become ill. I helped her sit and said, "Rose, what is it? Should I call Doctor Menschyk?"

She didn't say anything right away, but took my hand and patted it. Then she said, "No, Ida, thank you. I'm quite all right. I just had a little shock, is all."

"A shock? What kind of shock?"

"It was her. I recognized her voice."

"Whose voice?"

"The woman I heard in Pupik's office.

"It was Maria!"

****

When Mrs. K had recovered sufficiently, we continued on to breakfast. Neither of us knew what to say about what we had just learned. It only complicated the dilemma we had already been facing: What do we do about it, if anything; whom do we tell, if anyone. I mean, could we really keep this all to ourselves?

"Ida," Mrs. K said when we were finished breakfast, "I think we need to know more about this Maria than what Naomi has told us and what we have found out about the casino and Pupik. And I think I know the place to start."

"And that is where?"

"With the person who knows her best. Or at least should know her best. Her husband."

"You mean the man who gives the massages? What is his name? Jim?"

"I think it is John," Mrs. K said.

"And how will you get this information from him?"

"The easiest way, I think, would be to schedule a massage from him."

I was a little surprised. I have had a massage or two over the years, though not lately, and I liked it well enough. But I was sure Mrs. K had told me she disliked the idea, although she had never tried it.

"If I remember right," I said, "you thought it's like paying someone to cover you with *schmaltz*" (that's chicken fat) "and then give you a squeeze here and a *patch* there."

Mrs. K laughed. "Yes, Ida, and I still think so. But I'm sure I can stand it this once, in a good cause. And besides, I've heard several of the residents say they really enjoy getting a massage and they do it every week, so maybe it won't be at all bad."

Mrs. K went to telephone this John Cartwright and make an appointment. She returned a few minutes later and said, "I was in luck, Ida. Mr. Cartwright had an opening this afternoon, at 2:30."

"*Mazel tov.* And tell him to go easy on the *schmaltz.* You don't want to slide right out of your clothes when you're finished."

****

So at 2:30, Mrs. K knocked on the door of the little room where John Cartwright gave his massages, and at 3:30 I met her as she left the room. She looked a little worn out, and she was definitely *farshtunken*—she gave off quite an aroma. Whatever Cartwright put on her body, even if it wasn't really *schmaltz*, it smelled almost as bad. Like flowers that had been left out in the sun too long.

I of course asked her what had happened, but she waved her hand at me and said, "A shower first I need, then we can talk. I shall meet you in the lounge in a half hour."

And she walked straight to her apartment. A *bissel* wobbly, perhaps, but almost straight.

****

"John Cartwright seemed like a nice enough man," Mrs. K began when we had served ourselves tea and found a comfortable seat in the lounge. She looked and smelled a lot better than when I had last seen her.

"He first had me sign a paper of some sort saying I was in good health and it was okay that he should touch me."

"I guess that makes sense," I said. "Someone might say he touched them without their permission, and then he would be, what is it, up the creek without a rowboat."

"A paddle, Ida, but yes, it seems everything we do these days someone is asking that we agree they are not responsible for it. Anyway, I signed and then he asked me would I like to take off all my clothes."

"All your clothes? You should be naked?"

"Yes, apparently that's quite common. You're covered by a sheet, of course, but that's all."

"And what did you say?"

"I said I would prefer not, and he said that was perfectly all right and I could keep on my underwear. He then asked me what kind of massage I wanted—I didn't know there were different kinds—and I said just something to help me relax, and he said that was fine and asked me to get undressed. There was a screen behind which I took off my dress, and a robe to put on. Then I lay down on this special table with a thing like a bagel at one end and put my face in the bagel."

"Yes, I remember those tables. What happened then?"

"Well, he spread something oily on my back, something that smelled like a *mishmash* of fruits and flowers and spices, which you probably could smell when you met me, and he started to push me here and squeeze me there. Actually it felt pretty good—he had a very light touch and clearly knows what he is doing."

"Yes, I'm glad you were enjoying yourself. But of course that's not why you were there. Did you find out anything about his wife Maria?"

"I was getting to that. With my face in the bagel, it was hard to have a conversation with him, but about halfway through the hour he had me turn over and lie on my back. Then I was able to talk to him."

"What did you say?"

"I said I understood he was married to the lady who takes care of Miriam Blumenthal, and how convenient it must be to both be working in the same place. I asked a few questions like how long they had been married, how they had met, you know."

"And he was willing to answer such questions from a stranger?"

"Well, perhaps he wanted to tell someone, and I reminded him of his mother or a favorite aunt; or perhaps he thought I was just being a nosy old lady and was too polite to tell me to mind my own business."

"So did you learn anything interesting? Anything that might help us deal with Naomi's problem?"

"I'm not sure, though I did learn a lot. He told me how they met—apparently she had been married to a good friend of his. She began flirting with John, which led to something more … more intimate, and soon her marriage was *kaput*. After she divorced her husband, John started to go out with her. Even then, he said he thinks she was seeing other men—apparently one or two at a time are not sufficient for her—but he must have been willing to overlook that because eventually they got married. I think he is her third husband already."

"She has a collection?"

"It seems that way. I got the impression Maria is a bit loose in her morals."

"To say the least. And that certainly fits in with her fooling around with Pupik."

"Yes, and it doesn't speak well of her character in general, does it?"

"Do you think that means she is more likely to be taking advantage of Miriam?"

"I would say so. Whatever else Maria is, trustworthy she is not. And there was one other thing I learned."

"What was that?"

"Although he spoke as if he didn't really mind it, I had the distinct impression from his tone of voice—and from how much harder he squeezed my foot—when he was telling me about how Maria so easily plays around with other men, that he doesn't like it at all, now that he's her husband."

I nodded agreement. "I can't blame him, even if he was previously the one with whom she played. Now the shoe is on the other foot."

"Exactly. I don't think he trusts her, and probably with good reason. You know what they say: *Ven a ganef kusht, darf men zikh di tseyn ibertseyln.*

"When a thief kisses you, count your teeth."

Chapter 10

Mrs. K and I had still not had a talk with Miriam since Naomi asked us to look into her relationship with Maria Cartwright. You'll recall that when we went to see her, she was out, and then we "tailed" her to the casino. The next time we saw her, she was with Maria. So we decided to try once more to have that talk.

We again knocked on Miriam's door, and this time we were successful. We heard her coming slowly to the door.

She opened the door and greeted us warmly. She was in her wheelchair, but her apartment was equipped specially for a handicapped person, so it didn't stop her from getting around like anyone else.

Miriam is one of those people who can seem quite severe sometimes, almost unfriendly. But at other times, she is a very genial person, especially in the company of friends. So she gave us a nice smile and invited us in.

I guess you would say Miriam's apartment fitted her personality, because it too was severe: There was little decoration, and what there was, you would not call cheerful or colorful. There were a few paintings on the walls, but they were in dark colors. I couldn't tell you what they were paintings of, because they were mostly a *mishmash* of lines and blotches, as if the artist had forgotten what he was trying to paint halfway through the job. *Nu,* it seems to me art is whatever you think it is, even if other people think it is rubbish.

"It's nice to see you both," Miriam said after we had seated ourselves in straight-backed chairs that were on one side of a coffee table—there was no sofa. Miriam sat in her wheelchair facing us, and said, "Can I get you some tea or coffee?"

Mrs. K declined the offer, and although I could have used a nice cup of tea, I understood that Mrs. K wanted to get right to the matter we came about, so I declined also.

"So what brings you here?" Miriam asked. "Not that you have to have a reason to visit."

"We happened to be talking with Naomi," Mrs. K said, "and we were reminded how long it's been since we had visited with you. So here we are."

"I see," Miriam said. "Well, it's nice of you to drop by. I agree it's been a long time since we just chatted."

We made with small talk for several minutes, as was only polite, and then Mrs. K steered the conversation in the direction she wanted it to take.

"So Miriam," Mrs. K began, "how are you getting along with your … what is she called … your companion?"

"You mean Maria?" Miriam said. "Just fine, I guess. Why do you ask?"

"No reason," Mrs. K said, which of course was not true. I'm sure she simply wanted to see Miriam's reaction.

"What is it she does for you?" she asked next. "Does she help you with dressing? Does she take you places?" This, of course, was the big question we came to ask.

Miriam said, "Oh, yes. She does all of that. That is, when I need it. I can actually get along quite well in the morning if I have to, but having Maria here makes things a whole lot easier. As for taking me places, she drives me to the park, to the movies sometimes, you know."

This was just what she had told Naomi and Naomi told us. Perhaps it was mostly true, but we now knew it was not the whole story.

Just about then, I noticed something on a lamp table nearby that I thought I recognized. I wanted to get Mrs. K to look also, but I couldn't just tell her in front of Miriam. Then I had an idea how to do this.

"Miriam," I said when there was a pause in the conversation, "I think I really would like that cup of tea you offered. My throat is feeling a little dry, maybe from the weather. Would you mind?"

"Not at all, Ida. I'll just go and put the kettle on." She left the room. As soon as she was gone, I leaned over and whispered to Mrs. K, "Look, Rose. Over on that table. Is it what I think it is?"

Mrs. K looked where I was indicating. She adjusted her glasses and finally said, "Yes, I believe it is. Hmm. Let me think how to handle this."

Mrs. K was doing her thinking when Miriam returned with a tray with a teapot and three cups—a good hostess does not let her guests eat or drink alone—and a plate of little *rugelach*, which are traditional Jewish cookies. Very rich pastry, cut in triangles and rolled with fruit or nuts or even chocolate. Difficult to resist.

We sipped and munched for several minutes. Then Mrs. K, acting as if she had just noticed the object we were looking at, said, "Miriam, is that one of those tokens they use instead of coins at the casino down the highway? Someone showed me one the other day, and it looked just like that. Do you ever go to the casino? I understand it's quite an interesting place."

"Why … why no. No, someone must have accidentally left it there—I hadn't noticed. No, I've never been there. To the casino, that is."

Clearly Miriam was very uncomfortable and trying hard to make this token seem unimportant. In the process she was making it seem very important indeed.

Mrs. K did not pursue the matter further, for which I am sure Miriam was most grateful. There was more conversation about the upcoming holiday and the planned Purim play. Mrs K tried to ask again about what she and Maria did when they left the Home, but Miriam changed the subject. After a few more minutes of *shmoosing*, Mrs. K and I thanked Miriam for the tea and the hospitality and excused ourselves.

"It's been nice catching up, Miriam," Mrs. K said. "We should do it more often."

I am not so certain Miriam agreed.

****

Back in Mrs. K's apartment, we discussed what had just happened.

"Ida, it's clear Miriam is not comfortable talking about her activities with Maria Cartwright, at least about the casino visits."

"She certainly didn't want us to think she'd been there. Do you think it might be a, you know, a guilty conscience?"

"Maybe. Perhaps her gambling is a little more serious issue with her than we had thought.

"I'm sure it would be to Naomi."

Chapter 11

We decided we would pursue Naomi's problem with Maria further as soon as we had the time. Meanwhile, however, there was work to do. It was now only two weeks before Purim, and although we had arranged for the costumes and the script, we still hadn't arranged for the people who would wear the costumes and act out the script. That was our next task; the rest would have to wait.

About a dozen of the residents had told Mrs. K after her announcement that they would help with the play. Not all were willing to be actors, but enough were so we could fill all the parts. There are only maybe five characters absolutely necessary in a Purim play, and also a narrator, so we would have enough actors. Everyone else could help with the costumes and decorations and ordering the food. There is always food. In this case, we would need to bake lots of *hamantaschen*: poppy seed (my favorite), apricot, and prune.

"So who is going to play Queen Esther?" Karen Friedlander asks as we are eating our grapefruit. Queen Esther, sometimes called Hadassah, is what you might call the main character in the play. The star of the show.

Mrs. K said, "Actually, I was thinking I would play Esther. I remember doing it when I was eleven or twelve and …"

"Wait a minute," interrupts Isaac Taubman, who is

71

usually not so rude. But he is smiling. "Queen Esther is supposed to be this beautiful young queen. Beauty is not a problem here, but young we no longer are."

"Of course," Mrs. K said. "But it is only a play. Remember, Queen Esther is usually played by a girl of ten or twelve. Or maybe only six or seven, depending on which Sunday School class puts on the play. I am certain the Queen Esther in the *Megillah* was older than six or seven."

"And younger than sixty or seventy," Karen added, putting her two *shekels* in. Sometimes she can be a real pain in the *tuchis*.

"Yes, of course. But as there are no ladies here who are younger, or at least that much younger, we will make do with what we have."

So that was settled, since Mrs. K was organizing the whole event and therefore could decide who would play what.

"So Isaac, how about you playing King Ahashuerus?" Mrs. K said. "You get to have two beautiful ladies." She was referring to Queen Esther and Vashti, the former queen who disobeyed the king and was executed for her trouble.

Taubman's eyes got very wide. He laughed and said, "You make an offer it's hard to refuse. What would I have to do?"

"Just wear a costume—a crown and a robe is all it is—and read a few lines."

"Do I have to memorize a speech and act things out? I was never very good at that."

"No, you can hold the script in your hand if you want. And there is very little 'acting out' involved."

"Hmm. Now, if someone were to bribe me with an

offer of, say, a nice cinnamon babka …"

We all knew that Mrs. K makes the most delicious cinnamon babka.

Mrs. K laughed. "Okay. One cinnamon babka bribe. *Nu,* so you'll do it?"

Taubman thought it over and then said, "You've got yourself a king. Now is it okay if I finish my bagel?"

"Certainly, oh king," Mrs. K said with a little bow. We all laughed.

"And Karen," Mrs. K said, turning to her next victim, "would you like to be Queen Vashti?"

"You mean the one who gets executed?"

"Well, yes, but that does make it a shorter part. Less to do."

"What about Ida? You'll need a part for her," Karen said, obviously hoping to avoid getting involved. Actually, I was thinking the same thing: What about me?

"I think Ida should be the narrator," Mrs. K said. "I think she would be very good at telling the story. She is always telling people about our little … our little investigations." She turned to me and added, "Right, Ida?"

I had to admit she was right. So I became the narrator.

Karen finally agreed to be Vashti, as long as she did not have to take her clothes off and could be executed early in the proceedings, so she could sit down before her bunions began to hurt. To this Mrs. K readily agreed.

That only left finding who would play Mordecai and Haman. The *mensch* and the stinker.

I'll bet that nice Jewish boy Stevie Spielberg never had such a problem casting his pictures.

Chapter 12

Mrs. K lost no time in finding the rest of the cast. To play the evil Haman, she first approached Abe Wasserman. Perhaps you recall that is who we are calling "Little Wasserman," not to confuse him with "Big Wasserman," Jacob Wasserman. Jacob is tall, while Abe is short and round. The reason she thought of him in particular I don't know. Maybe it was because he fits her image of Haman better than most other residents. As I'm sure I once mentioned, it is Little Wasserman who enjoys staring at the *bristen* (the bosom) of Tiffany the *zaftik* manicurist while she bends over to give him a manicure. This is no big crime, of course, and Tiffany does go out of her way to display her, well, her wares, but it is at least slightly naughty, and so slightly over on Haman's side of the ledger.

Wasserman at first declined the invitation, but Mrs. K can be very persuasive, and anyway I think she offered to bake him some nice *mandelbrot*—those crispy almond cookies I mentioned before—and this he couldn't refuse. She'll be very busy in the kitchen after Purim.

That left only someone to play Mordecai, Esther's cousin and the leader of the Jews in the city of Shushan, where the Purim story takes place. For some reason it was easier to fill the part of the evil Haman than the *mensch* Mordecai. Maybe that's because it's easier to look and sound like a bad person than a good person. But finally Mrs. K convinced Mr. Sol Lipman to take the part. He owed her a favor, after she helped him deal with his wife Lily's *mishegoss*—her craziness—on more than one occasion. Like the time she locked herself in the bathroom and accused him of being a sex maniac. But that's another story.

Personally, I think it was to have an excuse to get away from Lily while rehearsing the play that Sol agreed. But you shouldn't tell him I said so.

It wasn't a problem to fill in the more minor parts in the play, and within a few days we were ready to rehearse.

Just like real actors.

****

It was Thursday afternoon, and the first rehearsal was about to begin, when Sol Lipman came to Mrs. K looking like a school boy who had *pished* his pants. Uncomfortable and embarrassed.

"I don't know how to tell you this, Rose," he said, looking down at his shoes as if he had a speech written on the toes, "but I can't be in the Purim play after all."

This was quite a surprise, and not a good one.

"I don't understand," Mrs. K said. "How is it yesterday you could do it, and today you cannot? Are you ill? Is there something wrong with your voice?"

"It's not my voice there is something wrong with," Sol said quietly, "but my wife."

Mrs. K and I looked at each other. Sol is a *mensch*, a nice man and a gentleman. Everyone likes Sol. Everyone, apparently, except Lily. Or so it sometimes seems, because hardly a week goes by when Lily is not making life difficult for her husband. And whereas Sol is a calm, soft-spoken man, Lily is high-strung like one of

75

those yappy little dogs and prone to screaming, mostly at Sol. We all wonder how the poor *schlemazl* stands it. Or why. But they say opposites attract, so …

Anyway, Sol explained: "When I told Lily about taking the part of Mordecai, she said I just wanted to be able to fool around with the ladies in the play—I guess that would be you and Ida and, who else? Is it Karen? She's always been jealous, but this is ridiculous!"

"Yes," said Mrs. K, "it is. But maybe we can find a way to deal with it." We all thought for a while, until Mrs. K brightened and said, "How about we also offer Lily a part in the play? That way she can keep an eye on Sol and we can get on with our rehearsals."

Sol did not look hopeful. "I don't know, Rose," he said, "Lily really isn't the acting type. More the sit-in-the-audience-and-*kibbitz* type."

"Hmm. Maybe we will have to induce her. Give her a big part."

"She could be Vashti," I said. "Karen really didn't seem to want to do it, and to be honest, Lily has just the personality for it, someone who is so stubborn her husband executes her and marries a more agreeable woman."

Immediately after saying this I was afraid maybe I had offended Sol by describing his wife that way. I think it sounded worse than I meant it—I actually like Lily, even if she can be a pain in the *tuchis* for poor Sol. But rather than seeming offended, Sol smiled and said, "Yes, it does seem the perfect part. And she is definitely one who would rather be executed than appear in public with no clothes on. Do you think I can convince her to do it?"

I was skeptical, knowing Lily to be a very private kind of person, but Mrs. K was much more positive about it. "I think you can," she told Sol. "Tell her how much we want her to join us, and that she will then be in the perfect position to watch that you don't, as you said, 'fool around.'"

So Sol went off to find Lily and see if he could talk her into playing the part of Queen Vashti. In the meantime, we all took a break and Mrs. K and I sat down in the lounge and poured ourselves some hot tea.

"Did I tell you, Ida, about seeing Sol in the garden the other day?" Mrs. K asked as we sipped our tea.

"I don't think so," I said. "But that seems hardly worth mentioning."

"Well, ordinarily, yes. But it was another example of the … shall we say, difficult relationship between Sol and Lily."

"*Nu,* so what happened?"

"I wanted to cut a few flowers for the vase in the living room," Mrs. K said, "so like usual I went out in the garden with my clippers." We have a big garden with lots of nice flower bushes. The Home allows residents to cut some flowers to enjoy in their rooms, as long as no one takes too many, of course. Almost no one takes advantage of this, but Mrs. K always likes to have fresh flowers whenever they are available.

"As you know, in March there are not a lot of flowers to choose from, so I was all the way at the back where we have some nice forsythia," Mrs. K said. "And there I see a long trail of smoke coming from behind one of the bushes. This seems strange, so I walk over and look behind the bush and who do you think I see there?"

"I can only assume it was Sol Lipman," I said, "since you already told me this is a story about seeing Sol in the garden."

"Yes, of course. And he was smoking a very large cigar. I asked him why out here, and in the cold? You can probably guess what he said."

And of course I could. "He was hiding from Lily, correct?"

"Correct. He said Lily hates the smell of cigars—I cannot say I blame her, so do I—but Sol enjoys smoking a cigar once in a while, so once in a while he smokes one outside."

"So what's so interesting about this?" I asked.

"What is interesting is that Lily not only does not let Sol smoke inside, but she does not let him smoke outside either. 'Please do not say anything to Lily,' he said. 'I'll never hear the last of it.' He looked really worried. It turns out if Lily finds out he's been smoking, wherever he does it, she'll *nudjen* poor Sol for a week. So he not only has to smoke outside, but he has to hide while he does it."

"Poor Sol. I assume you will keep his little secret?"

"Of course. Openness and honesty may be very important in a marriage, but sometimes it's much more important what the spouse does not know than what they do. As the saying goes, 'Ignorance is bliss,' although in Sol's case, I doubt their marriage could ever be called blissful."

I suddenly thought of the marriage of Maria and John Cartwright. If we were correct about what Maria has been up to, you can be sure she does not want her husband to know about it. There would be more than just cigar smoke between them if he ever found out. I would want to be farther away than the garden on that occasion.

So just as Sol has to hide his secret smoking from Lily, no doubt Maria goes to some trouble to hide her indiscretion from her husband John. And the same, of course, would apply to Pupik and his wife Margaret, although Sol's "sin" is of course far less serious than Maria's or Pupik's. So much deception in what should be a trusting relationship.

Just then the person in question, Sol Lipman, returned, and he was accompanied by Lily.

"Lily has agreed to be Queen Vashti," Sol announced, and Lily actually looked pleased to have been asked.

Go figure.

And within a half hour we were all rehearsing, including both Sol and Lily. Karen Friedlander had gladly changed to a more minor part, and so everyone was happy.

Well, "happy" might not describe Lily at the best of times, but this was as close as she was liable to come.

Another problem I'll bet Stevie Spielberg never had!

Chapter 13

Finally Sunday, the day of our Purim play, arrived. Mrs. K and I had made sure everyone at the Home knew about it and planned to attend. We had urged everyone to come in some kind of Purim costume, even if only a mask, and a bit to our surprise almost everyone did, including the staff. Many had made robes out of sheets or three-cornered Haman's hats out of cardboard, with the help of Gwen, the Home's crafts instructor, who made it one of her projects for the week. In fact, with everyone in a mask and maybe a costume, it was difficult or impossible to tell who was who, even whether they were a man or a woman, which added to the enjoyment.

The play was held in the dining room, which had been cleared of tables. With a combination of dining chairs and extra folding chairs, they were able to seat maybe a hundred and fifty people, including many of the residents' children and grandchildren. Everyone was in a holiday mood. Our activity director, Martha, who had helped with all the preparations, passed out *groggers* to everyone. She had us try them out a few times, and such a racket it made you could hear nothing else until it stopped.

I have already described briefly the story of Purim. For the whole story you should read the Book of Esther, which, as I have said, we call the *Megillah*. In the play, as narrator I read from the script, and as I got to each part of the action, such as Queen Vashti refusing the summons of King Ahasuerus to appear before him and his friends wearing nothing except her crown, the players would act out that scene. So in this case, Lily Lipman, playing Vashti, tore up the King's note summoning her. (Just between us, I am certain we all were grateful that she didn't decide to obey the King's order. The sight of Lily wearing only a crown on her head might well have emptied the dining room before we could finish the play.)

We did not act out the King executing Vashti, as we thought Lily might object. And besides, some scholars say Vashti was only banished. So we banished her to behind the curtain.

And of course every time there was mentioned the name of Haman, the King's evil advisor—and it was mentioned quite often—everyone whirled around their *groggers,* making such a noise it was difficult for a person to think, much less hear. *Oy,* the *tumel*! But of course that was the idea.

****

As I said, nearly all the residents were at the play. We had even seen Maria pushing Miriam in her wheelchair toward the dining room, both wearing little masks. But I didn't remember seeing them in the audience.

As soon as the play was over, the audience gave us some nice applause and spins with their *groggers*. Again a terrible noise, but it meant they enjoyed the play, so we didn't mind. After taking a bow, Mrs. K and I quickly walked to the back of the dining room, where there is the kitchen, because the staff, who were also out front watching the play, had earlier prepared trays of *hamantaschen* for everyone to enjoy, and we wanted to help bring them out.

We were the first ones to reach the kitchen. We pushed open the swinging doors. There seemed to be no one there, at least until we looked down.

What we saw there instantly turned our celebration upside down.

Lying on the floor, on her back, was a woman, and on her clothes was a red stain that was getting bigger and bigger.

On closer inspection, we saw that the woman was Miriam's helper, Maria.

And there was no doubt she was dead. Very much dead.

But then the even bigger shock: Standing over her, wearing a King Ahasuerus costume and holding in his hand a small gun, was none other than that *momzer* Pupik, general manager of the Julius and Rebecca Cohen Home for Jewish Seniors.

Chapter 14

"Got in himmel!" cried Mrs. K. God in heaven. I could say nothing. I was feeling faint and turned away. Poor Karen Friedlander, who had just entered the kitchen and has a somewhat delicate constitution, did faint. One of the kitchen staff hurried over to give her some water.

"Murder," someone cried, and the word worked its way around the room.

We simply could not believe what we were seeing. A woman murdered right here in the kitchen of the Home, and during such a happy occasion as Purim, would have been enough of a shock. But that the victim was Miriam's companion, and Pupik was the one who shot her—*oy gevalt,* it was almost too much to take in at one time.

You're probably wondering what Pupik was doing while we were all staring at this scene from out of a murder mystery story. He had taken his mask off, so we could see his face, which seemed to be without any color at all. At first he just stood there, like a statue, still holding the gun. But then he looked around and seemed for the first time to notice all of us watching. The look on his face was, as they say, like a deer caught in the headlights. He looked down at the gun in his hand, dropped it on the floor, turned, pushed his way through what was by now a good-sized crowd, and left the kitchen. No one tried to stop him.

Mrs. K, having recovered from her initial shock, asked the first important question of what would be many: "Where is Miriam?"

Where indeed. The last we had seen of Maria—at least the last we had seen her alive—she had been pushing Miriam in her wheelchair. Now there was no sign of either the woman or the wheelchair.

No sign, that is, until someone shouted from the back of the kitchen, "It's Miriam. She's back here. She's fainted!"

Everyone rushed toward the back, and there indeed was Miriam, slumped over in her wheelchair like she was asleep. Someone ran to get a glass of cold water, while another person got behind her wheelchair and pushed her a few feet into a less crowded area, with more air. The person with the water threw some in her face. It seemed to revive her, but only slowly did she seem to recognize where she was.

"What happened?" she said in a very weak voice. Then she said more loudly, as if just remembering it, "Maria! Is Maria all right? Did I just dream it?" She was very agitated.

Mrs. K went over and said quietly to Miriam, "What did you dream? Maria has had an accident. Is that what you dreamed?"

Miriam's voice rose. "No," she said, "I dreamed someone came into the kitchen and shot her with a gun. Am I going crazy?"

She then took Mrs. K's hand and squeezed it and, looking up at her, asked, "Did it really happen? Please tell me it was only a dream." It was heartbreaking to hear her almost pleading with Mrs. K to tell her it didn't really happen. I'm sure Mrs. K wished she could.

Unfortunately, she could not.

"Yes, I'm afraid that's what happened," she said. She then began to stroke Miriam's hair, as Miriam covered her face with her hands and began to cry. The rest of the people moved away to give her some privacy, until only she and Mrs. K and I were at the back of the kitchen. Everyone else had gathered at the front, where of course there was still a dead body on the floor. It's strange how people are unable to resist watching terrible tragedies, like car accidents and train wrecks. Myself, I have seen enough tragedies in my life, and not on purpose, that I don't need to see any more.

Miriam seemed to have pulled herself together a bit and stopped crying. She had taken out a tissue and was wiping her eyes.

I guess Mrs. K decided this was a good time to find out just what had occurred, before the police and who knows who else arrived.

"Tell me what happened," Mrs. K said in a quiet voice. "How did you happen to be back here and Maria up there?"

Miriam, still clinging to Mrs. K's hand, said, "I had asked Maria to bring me into the kitchen because the noise from the *groggers* was hurting my ears and I thought it would be a little quieter in here."

"Yes," I said, "It was getting pretty loud."

"So we were at the front of the kitchen, over there," and she indicated with her free hand the general area where we had found Maria.

"And there was this delicious aroma coming from the *hamantaschen* they had just baked," Miriam continued.

I looked around to where we had first found Miriam,

and there were indeed several trays with *hamantachen* that looked like they had just been taken out of the oven, set out to cool on a counter in the back of the kitchen by the oven. Apparently whoever had baked them had left them there and gone out to watch the end of the play. And now that the excitement had died down a little, I noticed the aroma too. It was hard not to reach over and have a little *nosh*.

That must have been how Miriam had felt, because she said, "I left Maria, who was watching the Purim play through the glass in the kitchen door, and pushed myself back here, thinking I would try a *hamantasch* while they were still warm. I made my way over there, where the trays are," pointing to the other end of the aisle, "but before I could take one, there was a terrible noise, like a gun going off, at the front of the kitchen. I looked up, and … and …" She stopped talking and began to sniff again.

Mrs. K let her rest for a moment, then she asked, "Did you see who it was who shot Maria?" This, of course, although the natural thing to ask at such a time, was really unnecessary in this case, as we all saw who was holding the gun that shot poor Maria.

Miriam shook her head and said, "No, I can't even say if it was a man or a woman. All I saw was someone … someone in a Purim costume holding a gun. And … and Maria on the floor in front of them. It was horrible. Like a nightmare. I guess that's when … when I fainted."

"*Got in himmel,*" whispered Mrs. K, for perhaps the third time since we arrived there. She turned and looked out toward the front of the kitchen. She then went over to where Miriam had indicated and looked out toward the front of the kitchen for a minute or so, saying nothing, bending down a little to get a better view, then walked slowly back to where I was still standing with Miriam.

We all had puzzled expressions. How could one not be puzzled, that Pupik's relationship with Maria should end in such an *umglich*, such a tragedy?

How did an affair turn into murder?

****

By now someone had called Dr. Arnold Menschyk, the doctor who looks after most of the residents at the Home. He arrived, out of breath, carrying his black doctor's bag. (Menschyk is probably one of the few doctors who still makes house calls, for the simple reason many of the residents of the Home are in no condition to call at his office. It comes with the territory, he once remarked to me.)

It did not take Menschyk long to determine that Maria was dead—we really didn't need him to tell us that, although of course it's necessary to get the official proclamation, so to speak. After kneeling down and examining her, Menschyk rose and looked around at all of us watching. He just shook his head sadly. I'm sure he would have said something like, "Someone call the police," but we all could already hear the sirens. They kept getting louder, as if to emphasize the extent of this tragedy.

The police would be here soon enough.

But at least this time, I thought, there would be no need for Mrs. K to get involved and to solve another mystery. We had all seen for ourselves who was responsible for this terrible thing. It was, as they say, an open and shut case.

Open, yes. Shut, it turns out, not so much.

Chapter 15

The police who arrived seemed to be just the ordinary patrolmen who drive around in the black and white cars. I was hoping Benjamin, Isaac Taubman's son, who is a policeman—*oy,* he always looks so smart in his uniform with the shiny gold buttons—would be one of the officers who came in, but he was not. It was just a thin, middle-aged young woman with brown hair and an older, more stocky man with a moustache but almost no hair at all. They took statements from everyone, and in the meantime a young woman not in a uniform came and took pictures of the scene. Then an ambulance arrived and they took poor Maria away. In and out came and went the police, and we all just watched and kept out of their way.

One of the officers, the man, took out a notebook and asked several of us what had happened. We described what we had seen, and of course they then went to find Pupik, who had apparently gone to his office, or so someone who had seen him said.

The next thing we all saw was Pupik being led away between the two police officers who had arrived first. He looked about as miserable as it is possible to look, and I have to admit that I felt sorry for the *schlemiel.*

I said as much to Mrs. K, who replied, "Yes, I do too, that he should have been driven to do such a terrible thing. But I think I feel even more sorry for poor

Margaret. Can you imagine finding out that not only has your husband been cheating on you, but now he's committed murder!"

I nodded in agreement. What a catastrophe!

****

When everyone, including the police, had left the kitchen and there was no more commotion, I said to Mrs. K we should go back to her apartment. I needed to sit down and recover from the shock of what we saw. Mrs. K, who had returned to the back of the kitchen to look around again, came back to where I was standing, shaking her head a little.

"It's all so strange," she said. "I don't understand."

"Neither do I," I said, and we left the kitchen together.

So we walked to Mrs. K's apartment, where she made some strong tea, and we sat and sipped a few minutes with our own thoughts before we got to discussing what had just happened.

Mrs. K spoke first. She had been looking like someone trying to understand a puzzle and having no success. I soon found out why.

"Do you think, Ida, that if we had gone to Pupik and told him what I heard, he would have been forced to break off this … this adultery? And knowing that we knew, he would not have had the nerve to harm Maria."

I thought about this for a minute before answering.

"This is easy to say now," I replied, "because we've seen what happened. But at the time, you'll remember, we thought it was best not to let either Pupik or Margaret know what we had overheard. Who knew it would end like this? We shouldn't use hindsight to blame ourselves for what we couldn't even imagine."

Mrs. K sighed. "You're right, of course," she said. "It's too late to change anything, and of no use to say 'if only.'"

And once again we needed a little *schnapps* in our tea.

****

So naturally the next day we are having another visit from the police. I mean this time the bigshots who wear the suits and ties, the detectives, not the ones in the uniforms like those who first arrived and took Pupik away.

This is not the first time the police detectives have been called to the Home, and it is not the first time this particular detective has visited us. I'm talking, of course, about that nice Detective Inspector Corcoran, who Mrs. K has more than once helped to solve mysterious deaths at the Home. It was Corcoran who knocked on Mrs. K's door just after lunch the day after Maria's death.

Mrs. K and I were sitting and *schmoosing* and again going over what we had seen and heard the day before when we heard the knocking. Mrs. K went to the door, and I followed part of the way. When Mrs. K opened the door, I can't say I was surprised to see Inspector Corcoran standing there, his hands folded in front of him and a nice smile on his face. But I was surprised that when I looked around I did not see his *shlumpy* assistant Sergeant Jenkins standing behind him, looking like he had just been shopping for a suit at the local Hadassah Thrift Store. On previous visits from Inspector Corcoran, Jenkins had always trailed along, taking notes or just looking bored or sleepy.

Instead of Jenkins, I saw a woman. And the contrast with Jenkins could not have been greater. She was as neat and buttoned-up as he was wrinkled and sloppy. And while Jenkins usually slouched and looked tired, this woman's lips were pursed, her dark eyes piercing, her shiny black hair in a severe bun, and her posture like a soldier at attention.

"Hello, Mrs. Kaplan," Corcoran said. "We meet again. May we come in?"

"Of course," Mrs. K said, stepping back to admit them. "It's always a pleasure to see you, Inspector, although usually the occasion hasn't been the most pleasant."

Corcoran stepped across the threshold, then turned to introduce his companion as she followed him in.

I have described Inspector Corcoran while relating other of Mrs. K's investigations, but I'll remind you that he is tall and dark and reminded Mrs. K and me of that Inspector Dalgleish that used to be on television. I think low-key and soft-spoken would describe his manner.

"Mrs. Kaplan, this is Cynthia Porter. Sergeant Porter will be working with me on this case."

"I'm very pleased to meet you," Mrs. K said, extending her hand. Porter shook hands with Mrs. K and nodded, but said nothing. Perhaps, I thought, she is, what do you call it, mute? Or she has a sore throat?

Corcoran then saw me standing there and said, "Hello, Mrs. Berkowitz. I didn't see you there. I hope you're well."

"Very well, thank you," I said.

"Cynthia, this is Ida Berkowitz," Corcoran said to the mute woman. "You'll recall I told you about Mrs. Kaplan and Mrs. Berkowitz and how they seem to know everything that's going on here at the Cohen Home."

Another nod from the silent one. Maybe a tiny smile.

We shook hands.

"Please come in and have a seat," Mrs. K said, and she led everyone into the living room.

"I'll just go and make some tea," she said as we seated ourselves, Corcoran and Porter on the sofa, me in a soft chair. While we waited for Mrs. K, Corcoran made small talk, asking how I was enjoying the weather, that sort of thing. Porter still said nothing.

A few minutes later, Mrs. K returned with tea and *mandelbrot.* "I brought some of these almond cookies that you liked so well the last time we … we visited together." She clearly was not sure how to characterize that last time, and I couldn't blame her. It probably would have sounded presumptuous—and been a bit embarrassing for Corcoran in front of this new assistant of his—if she had said something like "the last time I solved a case for you," or words to that effect, although that would have been an accurate description of what happened.

Corcoran took a cookie and said, "It's called *mandelbrot,* isn't it? I remember." (In fact, the last time he told us his grandmother was Jewish and used to bake them.) He then turned and held out the plate of cookies to the silent Porter and said, "They're really delicious. You should try one."

And what do you know, this woman actually spoke, although what she said was, "No, thank you. I never eat while on duty."

Now I've heard that policemen are not supposed to drink on duty—drink liquor, that is—I assume tea or a glass of orange juice is allowed—but never that they could not eat a cookie. Corcoran looked like he had not heard this either, but he just said, "Yes, well …" and put down the tray.

I was already liking the Porter woman better when she was mute.

****

"So how can we help you?" Mrs. K asked after the *mandelbrot* had been eaten and the tea cups set down on the table. I noticed Porter had not taken any tea, either.

Corcoran cleared his throat, and Porter took a pen and note pad out from her pocket.

"You know, of course, what happened yesterday," Corcoran said, speaking to both of us. "I understand you were among the first to discover the … uh … discover Mrs. Cartwright."

We both nodded.

"Naturally, we will be interviewing everyone who was present. You never know who might have seen or heard something important. But I wanted especially to speak with you two, because I know from our past … our past experience that no one knows the people and the personalities here better than you do."

"Oh, I wouldn't …" Mrs. K began to say, but Corcoran waved her off.

"Now, don't be modest, Mrs. Kaplan. I think you not only know who is who, but you understand the relationships among the various residents, at least most of them."

Mrs. K just nodded. It was true, of course, and modesty was unnecessary.

"But Inspector," I said, "since we all know who … who committed this terrible act, because we all saw him standing over Maria with the gun, is there really any need to ask a lot of questions? Can't you just tell a judge what happened and that's the end of it?"

Corcoran smiled. "I wish it were that easy," he said. "First of all, even if the case were that clear, we would still want to establish the circumstances of the crime, the motive, and so forth. For example, someone who kills another, even in plain sight of witnesses, might claim it was self-defense, or that he was not in his right mind, or that it was an accident."

"And is this what Pupik is saying?" Mrs. K asked. "That it was an accident or he was not in his right mind?"

"Not exactly," Corcoran said. "In fact, what he is saying is a bit unusual for a suspect who was observed by maybe a hundred people standing over a shooting victim holding the gun that killed her, a gun I might add that belongs to him.

"He claims he didn't do it."

Chapter 16

No one said anything for a few seconds. Then Mrs. K asked, "What do you mean, he didn't do it? He says he didn't shoot her at all? That we all didn't see what we thought we saw?"

"Well, no. He admits he was standing over Mrs. Cartwright holding the gun that killed her. But he says he entered the kitchen and found her lying on the floor, already shot. The gun was lying beside her, or to be more precise it was lying between him and her."

I was trying to picture this in my mind, as I'm sure Mrs. K was also.

"He says," Corcoran continued, "that he thought he recognized the gun as one of his—I take it he's something of a collector—and stupidly—that's his word—bent over and picked it up to look at it closer. That, of course, is when you folks walked in and found him holding it."

We needed at least a minute to digest what Corcoran had said.

"I see what you meant that it's not so simple a case," Mrs. K said. "Of course just his saying he didn't do it doesn't prove anything."

"Yes, but our just saying he did doesn't either. We need a lot more facts before we can prove we have the right person."

"So you're saying you aren't so confident he did it

now that you hear Pupik's story?" I asked.

Corcoran shook his head. "No, actually I'm pretty sure he did. I find his story much too, shall we say, convenient and difficult to believe. But it doesn't matter what I believe. My job is to learn the facts and draw a conclusion once those facts are known.

"And that's why we're here."

****

Mrs. K and I told Corcoran (and Porter, who was still scribbling her notes) what we had seen, about Maria lying there in the front of the kitchen and finding Miriam in the back.

When we were through with the telling, Corcoran asked, "Tell me something about Pupik. I've met him, of course, but in what you might call a business context, not as a resident under his management. And I'm sure you two know him as well as anyone here."

"I suppose that's true," Mrs. K said. "Except perhaps his secretary, Hilda. But of course her relationship with him is also quite different from ours."

I put in my two cents: "Yes, he has to be nice to her or she'll quit. He doesn't have to be nice to us, as most of us don't have another place to live."

Corcoran smiled. He said to the Porter woman, "I told you about the time Mrs. Kaplan herself was suspected of being responsible for a death here …" He stopped and turned to Mrs. K and said, "I'm still somewhat embarrassed about that, Mrs. Kaplan, but I think we've managed to get past it." She smiled and nodded in agreement. Then he continued to Porter: "Anyway, I recall that Mr. Pupik was, shall we say, quite ready to believe Mrs. Kaplan was at fault. So I would imagine the relationship between them is not the most friendly." Back to Mrs. K: "Is that a fair statement?"

Mrs. K nodded. "You could say we get along, because we have to, but neither of us would be on the other's list of favorite people."

I'm afraid at this time I might have muttered one of my mother's favorite Yiddish curses, a little more loudly than was polite: *Megulgl zol er vern in a henglaykhter: bay tog zol er hengen un bay nakht zol er brenen.* It means he should turn into a chandelier, so he will hang by day and burn by night. Fortunately, I'm sure the police officers did not understand. Mrs. K did and gave me a look.

"So given that you and he are not ... are not the best of friends, how would you describe his relationship with the residents in general? After all, he didn't accuse them all of murder." Smiling he said this last.

"No, of course not," Mrs. K said. "But Pupik doesn't get along with almost any of the residents. He's what you would call autocratic. He treats the residents almost like inmates in a prison. It's like he has to put up with us, but wishes we would go away. His main objective seems to be to spend as little money on taking care of the residents as possible." She told him about charging Miriam extra to have Maria as a helper.

"Always looking at the bottom line, eh?"

"Yes. In fact, I think that's the only line he looks at. Although I have to admit that sometimes he loosens the purse strings a little bit. Like just now, when we wanted to put on the Purim play. You know, what we were doing when poor Maria was ... was killed. He actually authorized us to spend some money on it. But that was an exception. We were a little surprised."

"Hmm. I see," said Corcoran. "Any reason you

know of for this … this exception?"

Mrs. K and I looked at each other. We were getting into some deeper water here. Should we mention about what we heard in Pupik's office? We didn't really know that he authorized the money because he suspected we knew about him and Maria. When we didn't answer right away, what Corcoran asked next pretty much forced the issue, as they say.

"Okay, we'll pass that for the moment. Let me ask you this: Can you think of any reason, apart from his apparent lack of affection for the residents in general, why Mr. Pupik would want to harm Mrs. Blumenthal's assistant? I assume he didn't know her personally—"

That did it. Mrs. K interrupted Corcoran right there.

"Inspector, there's something very important you need to know. Ordinarily it is something Ida and I would keep to ourselves, but under the circumstances …"

Corcoran looked at us with a serious expression, and Porter even stopped scribbling and looked up expectantly. Obviously Mrs. K had decided they had to know what we knew.

"Yes?" was all Corcoran said.

"As I said, ordinarily we would not mention this, but I'm afraid it is, as you would say, relevant to the case. We believe Pupik was having an affair with Maria Cartwright, and it was not … not going well."

Mrs. K then explained what she had heard at Pupik's office door, and about recognizing Maria's voice as the one arguing with Pupik. I added a few details too. Porter scribbled as fast as she could.

When we were finished telling, Corcoran kind of shook his head.

"Mrs. Kaplan, I'm sure you realize how important

what you just told us is to this case. I'm surprised you didn't mention it right away."

I think we both turned a little red in the face. Mrs. K certainly did.

"Of course we were going to tell you. It's just that … that it's hard to say something that it seems will condemn someone, even someone who is not a good person, like Pupik. And it seemed since we all saw him standing there with the gun … well, it might not even be necessary."

I had seldom seen Mrs. K looking—and sounding—so embarrassed.

Fortunately, Corcoran made things easier for us.

"Yes, I can understand. It's never easy to be the one to point the finger at another person, or to testify in court against them, especially when you might be the one responsible for their conviction. I actually admire your reluctance. I have no doubt you would have told us even if we hadn't asked directly. So please don't worry about it.

"But I do have to ask a few more questions."

As much I assumed.

"Now, Mrs. Kaplan, as I understand what you told me, from what you heard it would appear Mr. Pupik and a woman, whom you think from the voice you heard was Mrs. Cartwright, were having an affair."

"That's right," Mrs. K said.

"And it further appears that the woman wanted to end the affair, accusing Pupik of just wanting to … to get her into bed, I think you said. And Pupik did not want to end the affair, and even threatened her by saying she would 'regret' it. Is that correct?"

Mrs. K looked at me, then back at Corcoran and

nodded, saying, "That is what I heard."

"Have you got all that?" Corcoran asked Porter, who looked up from her pad and answered, "Yes."

"Good. Now from what you say, Mrs. Kaplan," Corcoran continued, "you seem pretty sure that the voices you heard were those of Mr. Pupik and Mrs. Cartwright. I assume you have heard Pupik's voice many times and would not be mistaken about that."

"Of course not," Mrs. K said. "And who else would be in his office? The cleaning lady?"

Corcoran laughed. "Exactly so, and so we'll take it as a given that it was him. But with respect to Mrs. Cartwright, it's not as simple. As I understand it, you did not recognize the woman's voice at the time you heard the argument, and you only heard Mrs. Cartwright's voice for the first time … it was how many days later?"

Mrs. K looked over at me and said, "What was it, Ida? A week later?"

I thought about all the things that had happened between Mrs. K hearing the argument in Pupik's office and our meeting Miriam and Maria in the hallway. Yes, it did seem like about a week, or at least several days, and I said so.

Corcoran nodded, then rubbed his chin and looked thoughtful. He said, "Hmm. And how certain are you that it was the same voice? After all, not only was it a week later, but the first time you heard it, it was through a closed door."

Mrs. K didn't answer right away. It had not occurred to me that she could be mistaken about the voice; and she seemed so certain when we spoke with Maria in the hallway. But when you stop to think about it, to identify someone by their voice a week after hearing it through a closed door did seem a *bissel* weak as evidence for a murder.

I assume Mrs. K was thinking along the same lines, because when she spoke it was with a definite note of uncertainty.

"I see what you mean, Inspector. I of course can't be sure Maria was the woman I heard in Pupik's office, although the voice was pretty distinctive and, because they were talking loudly, not difficult to hear. For now, I suppose, the best I can say is that I'm pretty sure it was her, but I couldn't honestly swear to it."

"And there's no need for you to do that at this time," Corcoran said. "What you've given us is a lead that we'll follow up. If Pupik was having an affair with Mrs. Cartwright, I'm sure there will be other evidence of it. We may also discover evidence of some motive other than breaking off an affair, something we have no way of knowing until we begin questioning the other residents and staff. And of course given the circumstances, the 'smoking gun,' so to speak, proving a motive is less important than when there is only circumstantial evidence of the killing itself."

"Inspector," Mrs. K said, "could you perhaps not tell Pupik that we told you about his affair with Maria—if it was Maria, as you say? I mean, unless you really have to …"

"Don't worry, Mrs. Kaplan," he replied. "For now, we won't approach Mr. Pupik about it at all. We'll see if we can gather the information in other ways, as I said. If and when we have more than just your somewhat … well, somewhat thin evidence of an affair, we'll broach it with him. And by then we may have sufficient other sources that we can leave you out, at least for the time being. Although I can't guarantee it, of course."

Mrs. K nodded, and I think we both understood. At some point Pupik might find out we … what do they say on television … we ratted on him. I suppose it couldn't be helped.

Corcoran stood up, stretched his arms a bit, and walked over to the window. He looked out at the back lawn and seemed to be thinking about something. When he turned around, he said, "Okay, so we know Pupik was found holding the gun, we may find he had a motive for harming Maria Cartwright, although we don't know of one for certain at this time, and it was even his gun that killed her. But he says he didn't shoot her, that he saw the gun on the floor and picked it up just before you all entered the kitchen. We of course have to consider the possibility that, however things may look at first glance, he's telling the truth."

I think I might have rolled my eyes a bit at this, because Corcoran looked directly at me as if to say, "Yes, we must, whatever you or I might think." And of course he was right.

So we considered.

"Now taking Pupik's statement at face value," Corcoran said, still looking at me, but then he turned to face everyone, "we have to ask ourselves who, other than Pupik himself, might have had a motive or reason to harm Mrs. Cartwright. Does either of you have any suggestions in this regard?"

Mrs. K looked over at me, and I looked away. We both knew the answer to that, and neither of us wanted to say it. Finally Mrs. K did the honors.

"Now, Inspector, I am only telling you this because I don't wish to keep anything back that might help with your investigation. But it in no way should be taken as my saying she had anything to do with this ..."

"Excuse me, Mrs. Kaplan," Corcoran said, "but who are we talking about here?"

I think Mrs. K was putting the cart before the donkey. Or is it the horse? You know what I mean.

"Why, Miriam's daughter Naomi, of course. Or didn't we mention her yet?"

Corcoran smiled and said, "No, I don't think you did. But please do."

"I'm sorry. I'll start over. Naomi Schwartz, who is the daughter of Miriam Blumenthal, has been very suspicious of Maria. She came to us quite upset, telling us she thought Maria was taking over her mother's life, telling her bad things about Naomi and her brother, and perhaps trying to get money from her, money that Naomi thinks is rightfully hers and the rest of the family's. Naomi said her mother's present mental state is such that she would not be able to resist such a ... a bad woman. So she asked us if we would speak with her mother about it, perhaps find out what Maria was telling Miriam."

"Hmm. And did you speak with her mother?"

"Yes, eventually, but we really didn't learn anything important. We did follow her one day when Maria took her to the casino down the road—the Red Feather, I think it's called—but that's about all."

"So this Naomi was concerned about Maria Cartwright's relationship with her mother. Was this concern strong enough that she might have ... have wanted to harm Mrs. Cartwright?"

Again Mrs. K and I exchanged glances. But the truth was the truth.

"I'm sure she would never have done anything like

… like what happened, but yes, she felt very strongly against Maria and definitely would have liked to be rid of her."

"Her brother, Barry—Naomi's brother, that is, not Maria's—apparently was also very upset with Maria," I added. "He's something of a *kasnik.* A hot head." I'm sure the police would have found this out anyway, and I didn't want it to seem like Naomi was the only one who disliked Maria. On the other hand, I didn't think I needed to volunteer that Naomi said Barry would "do anything" to get rid of her. I'm sure he didn't mean shooting her.

Porter was again writing furiously.

Mrs. K nodded. "Yes, I imagine the entire family was watching what was going on between Miriam and Maria with … well, with apprehension."

Corcoran said, "Yes, I imagine so. We'll have a talk with all of them, of course. But it generally takes a lot more than apprehension to cause someone to murder another. Anyone else?"

I could not think of anyone offhand, but Mrs. K said, "Well, I would have imagined her—that is, Naomi's—husband, his name is Aaron, would feel the same as Naomi. But Naomi says he wasn't worried about Maria and had suggested the family leave her alone."

Porter wrote it down.

Mrs. K's mention of a husband reminded me of something.

"Speaking of husbands," I said, "I have heard that Maria and her husband were not getting along. The reason I don't know." It was from Mrs. Bissela, the Home's *yenta,* that I heard it, of course. I think I've mentioned Mrs. Bissela before. If at breakfast you say anything where Mrs. Bissela can hear it, you can be sure it will be common knowledge around the Home before lunch. And for her age she has very good hearing. "It is only a rumor," I added, and I was immediately sorry I had passed it on.

Corcoran asked what is the husband's name.

"John," Mrs. K said. "He's a massage therapist, I think it's called, and he comes here regularly to give residents massages. They are very helpful for all the aches and pains we tend to get.

"And perhaps it is more than a rumor."

Mrs. K then described briefly her massage appointment.

Corcoran smiled and nodded. Porter didn't smile and wrote.

"Is there anything else?" Corcoran asked.

Mrs. K and I both shook our heads. At least there was nothing else we thought the police needed to know.

Corcoran, who was still standing, walked over and shook hands with Mrs. K, and then with me.

"Ladies, I really appreciate your assistance," he said. "You've given us a good start on our investigation. If you think of anything else that might be helpful, please get in touch."

He took out two business cards and handed them to us.

"Just in case you've lost my number since the last time," he said with a nice smile. "But perhaps you have it memorized by now."

We all laughed at that. All except the Porter woman. Perhaps she considered it improper to smile on duty. Perhaps she had heartburn. Perhaps her *gatkes* were too tight. (Her long underwear it means.)

She would have been a lot happier if she had tried

the *mandelbrot*!

Chapter 17

We did not get in touch with the police the next day, but it was a real surprise who got in touch with us.

Mrs. K and I were just entering her apartment after breakfast when already ringing was the telephone. Mrs. K answered it before it could repeat itself. From her expression of surprise, she was not expecting to be talking to whoever it was on the other end. All I heard, though, was "Who did you say this is?" and "He what?" and "Are you sure?" Then there was a long silence as Mrs. K listened, looking at me with a puzzled expression.

"Well, certainly," she said, "I suppose we could … yes, today … where? … yes, we will see you then … goodbye." She made a note, hung up, and that was that.

"So *nu,* tell me already. Who was it, and what are we agreeing to do?"

Mrs. K was still standing by the phone, still looking puzzled, not an expression one usually associates with Mrs. K.

"You'll never guess who that was," she said.

"I'll take your word for it," I answered, "so I won't bother guessing. We can proceed right to the answer. Who was it?"

"It was Margaret, Pupik's wife. She asked if we would come to their home. Today."

Mrs. K had been right. I never would have guessed. Why would the wife of someone with whom the bad feeling is mutual, and who has just committed a murder, want to see us? I needed more information.

"Did she say why?"

"No, but she did say it was at Pupik's request that she called. He is the one who wants to see us."

This was now becoming truly *meshugeh.*

"He's at his home?" I knew he hadn't been at the Home since he was taken away by the police officers, and somehow I assumed he was in jail.

"Yes. Apparently he's out on bail."

"And you agreed to go?"

"You heard. Yes, and why not? Don't you want to find out why Pupik would want to see us?"

I had to admit I did.

"And so do I," Mrs. K said. "So this afternoon, right after lunch, we shall go and find out."

"I'm going to find it difficult to wait," I said. Which, when you think about it, is very strange, that we should be so anxious to see a man we have for years done our best to avoid seeing at all.

Go figure.

****

At two p.m., having given ourselves enough time to digest lunch before facing Pupik, we left the Home, headed for Pupik's house. We got his address from Hilda, who was back in Pupik's office, although he was not. A woman named Sonia Rothstein, his assistant manager, had taken over in his absence.

This time we took a taxi. No more roaring tigers, and no more bothering Sara and her boyfriends. Pupik lived what my son would call "way out in the boonies," whatever they are. It took almost half an hour to get there, but at least the ride was uneventful.

Pupik lived in a development called "Pleasant Acres." An interesting place for an unpleasant man to live, but never mind. The house turned out to be quite impressive, light brown and beige with two garage doors, three dormers, a large bay window, and a lovely garden in front, surrounded by a white picket fence that looked as if it had just been painted. Mrs. K paid the taxi driver (using our senior-citizen discount coupons, of course— it is a little enough benefit of getting old) and we passed through the gate in the fence and onto a cement path, painted pink, that led to two front steps. The front door, or rather the doors, as it was a double door, was itself imposing, being made of oak and beautifully carved with a geometric pattern.

"Pupik must do all right for himself." I said to Mrs. K.

"Yes," she said in a low voice, in case there was a Pupik on the other side of the door, "it's probably because he saves the company that owns the Home so much money, by spending as little as possible on the residents."

While she said this, Mrs. K was already pressing the doorbell button. What we heard was not a ringing bell, but a little melody, Mozart I think.

Fancy-shmancy.

In a few seconds, the door opens and there is Margaret Pupik, a woman we know only casually, having met her once or twice at some formal occasion, like the opening of a new wing at the Home. My impression of her, and I know Mrs. K's also, was of a very charming person, polite and soft-spoken, in fact just the opposite of her husband.

Looking at her, again I'm reminded that opposites

attract …

Nu, so there she was standing, a tallish woman of maybe five feet nine, slender, in her mid-fifties, with dark brown hair styled fashionably short. Her face, while a *bissel* on the long side to be what you would call pretty, was nevertheless attractive in its own way, perhaps because she smiled a lot.

But she was not smiling now, and her eyes were red and revealed the strain she must be under. I mean, how would you feel if your husband, supposedly an upright, if somewhat unpleasant, citizen was suddenly arrested for murder?

"Mrs. Kaplan, Mrs. Berkowitz," she said, smiling as best she could under the circumstances. "Thank you for coming. Please come in."

She stepped back and we entered a comfortable, well-lit foyer. A ceramic lamp stood on a table in one corner, and in another corner was an interesting sculpture that turned out to be a place to hang coats, which Margaret did with ours. She then ushered us into the living room, a large room with a deep pile carpet and furniture upholstered in a beautiful white and blue floral pattern. On the walls were large paintings, one on each wall, that could have come out of a museum. I guessed that it was more Margaret's taste than her husband's.

Margaret indicated we should sit on the sofa, and she took a seat on a matching chair across from us.

Apparently Margaret was going to tell us why we were there, before we would see Pupik.

When she did, it made her phone call asking us to come seem like nothing in comparison to our surprise when she told us why.

****

Margaret first offered us something to drink, which we both declined. I think we were too anxious to find out what this visit was all about.

Having done the necessary hostess thing, Margaret sat upright, cleared her throat, and began.

"I'm sure you know all about Harold's ... his situation," Margaret said. We both nodded. She was wringing her hands and was clearly very uncomfortable, but she went on. "They put him in jail, and we had to post a bond before they would release him. As it's a murder case, he could have been denied bail, but because of his long-time residence in the community and his record of good works and such, they apparently didn't consider him a threat to run away."

I was unaware Pupik had ever done any "good works," but of course I took her word for it. She continued:

"Still, we had to pay quite a lot for the bond, and the whole process was so demeaning, just like Harold was a common criminal."

Tears were forming in her eyes, and she dabbed at them with a handkerchief as she spoke. I felt so sorry for her, both for what she was going through and, to be honest, also for what she didn't know that we did. I'm sure Mrs. K was feeling the same way.

Just then, a very furry cat entered the room and jumped up onto Margaret's lap. She seemed grateful for the distraction and stroked it for a minute, until it decided it had had enough attention, jumped down and wandered off.

Margaret looked up and smiled. "Funny," she said, "Jasmine is usually quite aloof. I suppose she senses things are a bit ... a bit tense around here right now."

We nodded. How could they be any other way?

Margaret returned to what she had been saying. "We also had to hire a lawyer. A friend gave us the name of a good one, who specializes in … in murder cases. He will be very expensive, but what can we do? Anyway, when we got home from the … from the place where Harold had been kept, we first talked about what had happened, because of course I didn't know any of the details, just that he'd been arrested. Harold told me in no uncertain terms that he had not harmed Maria Cartwright, that he had come upon her lying on the floor of the kitchen, obviously … obviously dead. I mean she was bleeding, and …" Again she dabbed at her eyes, then took a deep breath.

Mrs. K said, "Take your time, Margaret. We know how hard this must be for you. Just tell us what you have to; you don't have to put in all the details."

Margaret gave a little smile back, took another deep breath, and said, "Harold says he almost fainted from the terrible sight and was about to turn around and get help, when he saw the gun lying on the floor by the … by her. He says it looked just like one of his special guns—he has a collection of guns, all kinds—and, without thinking, picked it up. Just then several people—I assume you two were among them—entered the kitchen and found him there, standing over Mrs. Cartwright and holding the gun. I think you know the rest—he dropped the gun and ran away."

Here she put her face in her hands and really did begin to cry. "He did everything wrong," she said between sobs. "Everything. And now … and now who knows what will happen?"

We let Margaret compose herself, which she soon

did, and then Mrs. K said, "We know this is a terrible situation for you both, but we are wondering why you called us out here to tell us. Or rather why your husband wanted us to come here." I nodded agreement. Why tell us?

"I'm sorry, I just wanted to be sure you knew Harold's side of the story. Why did he want you to come here? The answer is quite simple.

"He wants your help."

****

Now this was truly a surprise. As I'm sure I've mentioned more than once, the relationship between us and Pupik, and especially between Mrs. K and him, is not what you would call rosy. It's more what you would call a disaster. So why would Pupik be asking us for help? And why would we be offering him any if he asked? And what kind of help could we give him if we wanted to?

We were about to find out.

Mrs. K asked the first obvious question. "Why, if your husband wants our help—and I honestly don't know what sort of help he might have in mind—why does he not ask us for it himself?"

"Yes, I see," Margaret said. "I suppose it's because he's aware that you and he haven't always … gotten along. He thought perhaps if I explained his side of the story to you and sort of made the initial approach, there would be more chance of your agreeing. And he's been so upset, unable to sleep or eat, he said he just couldn't face you. I insisted that if he thought you could help him, he had to ask himself, but I agreed to speak to you first."

Just then I looked up and saw Pupik standing in the doorway to the living room. He looked entirely different from the last time I'd seen him—the last time before seeing him with the gun standing over Maria's body, that is—and the difference was not a good one. For one thing, he looked like he hadn't slept well in several days, which I'm sure he hadn't. Who would, under the circumstances? But he also didn't look "himself," if you know what I mean. The Pupik Mrs. K and I were used to always looked and sounded like he was doing you a favor just talking to you, like you were wasting his valuable time—as I've already mentioned, more like the warden in a prison than the manager of a retirement home.

But the man in the doorway was not the warden; he was the prisoner. And a beaten-down prisoner at that. If you'll pardon the bad word, he looked like he had been transformed from *shmuck* to *schlemazl*—from despicable person to luckless loser. Being arrested for murder will do that to a person, I'm sure. He also was dressed quite casually, in what they call leisure pants and a loose sweater, as one might who was just resting at home while getting over an illness. At the Home he was always impeccably dressed in suit and tie. Definitely a side of Pupik we had never before seen.

Mrs. K looked over to where my eyes were focused and, from the expression on her face, it was clear she also was struck by the change in Pupik. Margaret then rose and went over to her husband and said, gently, "Harold, I've told the ladies that you wanted them to help. Now I think you should sit down and explain."

Pupik nodded, then shuffled over in our direction. Mrs. K and I both rose, I'm not sure why, but he just went over to the chair that Margaret had vacated and sat down. We sat back down too, and for a moment no one spoke. Then Pupik looked at us both, managed a weak smile, and said, "Thank you, ladies, for coming. Please let me explain why I asked Margaret to contact you." His voice was low, but it was strong, like a person who knew exactly what he wanted to say.

So finally we were to find out what this was about. And from the horse's mouth, so to speak.

"I'm well aware," Pupik began, speaking slowly, as if choosing his words carefully, "that we have had our differences over the years. And I won't pretend that much of that isn't my fault. I have always taken my responsibilities at the Home very seriously— responsibilities, I might say, that I have to both the residents and the Home's board of directors—and sometimes I'm sure I have acted in a way that you or other residents felt was … was unfair, or unreasonable."

I would have liked to correct the "sometimes" part of this, but of course I didn't.

"And I also know I'm not always the easiest person to get along with," Pupik continued, and here he smiled and looked over at Margaret, who was standing in the doorway where Pupik had been and who also smiled. Just then, with the look on Margaret's face, I got the clear impression that, however many faults her husband might have, she was very fond of him and ready to forgive them.

"I've probably acted in some ways too authoritarian, and too lacking in sympathy for others, particularly the Home's residents. So it is, I suppose, a bit ironic that here I am, asking two of those residents for help. I wouldn't blame you if you refuse. But I nevertheless will ask."

"Just what kind of help do you have in mind?" Mrs. K asked when it appeared Pupik had come to the end of his speech. "I'm sure you have a good lawyer and …

well, friends who can help you."

"Yes, of course," Pupik said. "But the help I'm asking you for is quite different."

Pupik cleared his throat again and looked over at Margaret and asked her to bring him a glass of water. She nodded and left the room. We all waited until she returned with the water, asking us again if we wanted anything to drink, which we again declined.

After thanking her and drinking a few sips of water, Pupik put the glass down on the coffee table and continued. "I am, of course, aware of how you helped to … to get to the bottom, shall we say, of previous unexplained deaths at the Home. I know you've worked closely with the police, and to be quite frank, at the time I was not happy about your … about what I saw as your interference."

Considering that in one instance Mrs. K was attempting to avoid being charged with murder herself, in my opinion calling it "interference" took some *chutzpah*!

"But I'll be honest—I've been really impressed with your ability to learn the facts and to reach the right conclusions from them, something even the police seemed unable to do." Mrs. K had to smile at this admission. "And then, when I was being questioned by the police and told them my side of the story—I think Margaret has explained that to you—that police inspector—what is his name…"

"Inspector Corcoran?" Mrs. K said.

"Yes, Corcoran. That's him. He said to me—I don't know if he was serious—something like, 'What you need is to get Mrs. Kaplan to help you. If you didn't kill that woman, she'll find out who did.' I believe he even

116

compared you to Sherlock Holmes, who he said was your favorite detective."

This is of course true, and in telling these stories I like to think I am being her Dr. Watson.

"I didn't really focus on what he said at that moment," Pupik went on, "but after being in jail and here at home and having a lot of time to think about it, I'm sure that's exactly what I need."

"Even if you thought we were just 'interfering' in those other cases?" Mrs. K asked.

"Yes, I know. And how different things look when one is on the other side. But I'm being very honest here. Mrs. Kaplan, and you too, Mrs. Berkowitz, despite all of our differences in the past and regardless of what you think of me as general manager of the home, I need you to help me prove I did not kill Maria Cartwright. Because I did not. I swear I did not." This last was said with a great deal of emotion, despite Pupik's obviously weak condition.

And with that he stopped talking. He looked exhausted, and I'm sure he was. He sat back in his chair, sipped some more water, and waited for our answer.

And I am sitting there wishing we had one.

Chapter 18

Mrs. K and I looked at each other, and neither of us wanted to speak first. But finally she said, "Let me be sure I understand. You've said you didn't shoot Mrs. Cartwright—Maria—even though you were standing over her holding the gun that killed her. Is that right?"

"Yes, exactly. I found her lying there and—stupidly, I admit—picked up the gun."

"Because you thought it was yours?"

"Yes, at least it looked like one of mine. Turns out I was right, I guess."

"Do you have any idea who did kill her?"

"Absolutely not."

Mrs. K hesitated and looked over at me. I knew what she was thinking. I was glad I wasn't asking the next question.

"And do you … did you … have any reason to kill her?"

"Me? Why should I? I hardly knew her!" Pupik looked like he really didn't know, and I was reminded then of what Inspector Corcoran said. Is it possible Maria was not the woman in Pupik's office?

I'm sure Mrs. K was thinking the same thing, because she first glanced up at Margaret, who showed no sign that anything was wrong, and then said, "Mr. Pupik, I think it's necessary that Ida and I talk this over before we give you an answer."

Pupik shook his head a little. "Is it that you don't believe me? That you think I did kill that woman? I swear I didn't …"

"Not exactly," Mrs. K said. "It's a little more complicated than that."

What an awkward position we were in: We couldn't very well tell Pupik the real reason we doubted his story while Margaret was standing there and listening. And we couldn't agree to help him prove his innocence if he wouldn't admit Maria was his *tsastkele*. Unless, of course, Mrs. K had been mistaken and she wasn't.

What a mess. A real *kasheh*! (Think of buckwheat porridge, which the word also means, all mished up in a bowl, and you have some idea.)

"Perhaps you could excuse us for a few minutes while we talk this over," Mrs. K said. "It isn't as simple as if you were hiring a private detective, which I … which we are not. As you know, there were very good reasons we got involved in those other cases, and we would have to, well, to have very good reasons now too."

"Yes, I understand. Why don't Margaret and I leave you two to talk here, and you let us know when you've decided."

So Pupik and his wife left the room. Mrs. K looked at me and raised her eyebrows, enough to know she was thinking the same thing as I was:

Oy vey.

****

"So what do we tell Pupik?" I said very quietly. I didn't want that Pupik or Margaret—especially Margaret—should hear me. "That we only help people we think are innocent? Or that we like? Or that don't fool around with *ladies not their wife?"*

119

"Or that don't shoot them," Mrs. K added. "And if we did want to help Pupik, wouldn't we have to tell him we know about his *shtuping* Maria? And that we already told the police about it? But could we then keep it from Margaret?"

"So should we tell Pupik we can't help him, but not the reason?"

"It certainly would be less complicated that way. But what if he's innocent? What if his story is true, and someone else killed Maria? There were certainly enough other likely candidates for the job."

"Yes, that's true. We already thought of several without even trying."

We were silent for another minute or so, before Mrs. K looked up and said, "You know, Ida, it doesn't have to be that complicated. It's not as if we have to be working for one side or the other. We can tell Pupik that, although we of course do not know whether he's telling the truth, we'll make a few inquiries and see what we can find out, but that if what we find out points to him being guilty, then we will have to report that to the police."

And we wouldn't have to mention what we already found out and already reported to the police. I'm thinking this is as good a way around our problem as any, at least temporarily, and I say so. "We will be, what would you call it, independent private investigators. And we let the chips fall wherever … wherever they fall."

To tell the truth, I guess I was hoping Mrs. K and I would do a little snooping around. Things can get a *bissel* dull at the Home sometimes, and nothing livens things up like a murder.

If you know what I mean.

****

When Pupik and his wife came back into the living room, Mrs. K explained about being willing to look into the matter, without actually making any assumptions about who was or was not guilty. Pupik didn't seem happy with her answer, but there wasn't much he could do about it.

"I understand," he said. "You have no reason to believe my side of the story, and no particular reason to want to help me. But I'm sure you would want to know the truth, and I'm confident once you discover it you'll feel differently."

He asked Margaret to call a taxi for us and when it arrived they both thanked us for coming.

As we were leaving, Margaret opened the door for us and said softly, "We both appreciate your coming here, and that you'll be … be looking at this from a different perspective than the police. I know Harold will feel much better about things … he's been so depressed, and now he has a little more hope. Thank you."

In a way I wished she hadn't said that. We might think of ourselves as "independent private investigators," but if Pupik was thinking of us as his only hope, that put quite a weight on our shoulders.

Maybe more than we wanted to carry.

Chapter 19

Back at the Home, Mrs. K and I sat in the lounge and tried to understand how we had gotten ourselves into such a pickle. It was bad enough we had promised Naomi to help her to deal with a woman who had then been murdered. It was much worse that we somehow seemed to have aligned ourselves with the man who killed her. Or might have killed her. And we didn't even like the *momzer*.

"So, Rose, what do we do now? Are we supposed to start looking for ways to save Pupik from the police? How hard do we have to look?"

"I'm not quite sure," Mrs. K said. "I suppose we should at least do what we've done in the past to begin an investigation: Make a list of all the possible persons who might have committed the murder."

"A list of suspects, yes. Didn't we already give such a list to Inspector Corcoran?"

"We did. But we should write down the list for ourselves. Without it, we can't even begin to ask questions."

Mrs. K got up and said, "I'll go get a notepad."

While she was gone, I brought over a couple of cups of tea. We could hardly be expected to do our best thinking without tea.

Mrs. K returned a few minutes later with her notepad and a pencil. She opened the pad and said,

"Now, Ida, let's be as fair and open-minded about this as we can, regardless of what we saw and what we think of Pupik."

"That's a lot to be regardless of," I said. "It's like, what do they say, like ignoring the gorilla in the room."

"I think you mean the elephant. But yes, we'll just have to do our best. So let's start with the people we mentioned to Corcoran. I believe Naomi was first, for obvious reasons."

"Yes, Naomi, and her brother Barry—the whole family, in fact—except her husband, Aaron. Maybe they shot her together. Maybe …"

"Yes, thank you, Ida. Let's not get carried away."

"Still, it is strange, Aaron taking Maria's side. You don't suppose he and Maria … that they …"

"It's a possibility, I guess," Mrs. K said. "That would certainly affect the motives of a few people, wouldn't it? But somehow it doesn't seem likely."

I nodded. "So do you think Barry is the most likely of them? I mean, because he actually threatened to 'do anything' to stop Maria?"

"Personally," Mrs. K said, "I think he's all talk. Often those dogs who bark the loudest do the least biting."

"But didn't he once have a run-in with the police? I seem to remember something like that and how it upset Miriam."

"That's right. I think it was a bar fight, where he got into a brawl and they arrested him together with several others. I don't think he was actually convicted of anything."

"Maybe not," I said. "But still …"

"Still, it's not the same as committing murder, is it?"

Mrs. K obviously wanted to move on with the list. "So leaving Naomi's family," she said, "is there anyone else? I think we mentioned John, Maria's husband, to Corcoran, didn't we?"

"We did. Anyone else?"

We both thought about it. Of course, there could be a dozen people who we didn't know of who had some kind of grudge against Maria—she probably took advantage of more people than just Miriam—or people benefiting from Maria's will, that sort of thing, but since we had no way of knowing who they were, we would have to leave finding them to the police.

"What about Margaret?" Mrs. K asked.

"Pupik's wife? Why … oh, you mean if she knew about Pupik *shtuping* Maria and …"

"Well, we do have to look at all possibilities."

I agreed, but I thought that possibility was not worth spending too much time worrying about. Margaret didn't strike me as the kind of woman who would resort to murder, assuming she even knew about Pupik's affair, which I didn't think likely. But Mrs. K dutifully put the name down on her list. And I will admit it's hard to know how even the mildest person would react when faced with such a revelation.

"Anyone else?" Mrs. K asked. Neither of us could think of anyone else to put on the list.

"So what is our next step?" I asked.

But before she could answer, sitting down next to us was Mrs. Bissela, looking quite upset.

"*Nu*, Hannah," I said, "*vos makhst du?*"

"How should I be? A terrible thing, this killing, and right here at the Home."

We had to agree, of course.

"And at our Purim celebration yet," she continued. "Not that I was very fond of that Maria person, but …"

"Yes," Mrs. K said, "but no one would wish her killed like that."

Mrs. Bissela didn't respond right away, but she looked as if she didn't completely agree. It turned out she didn't.

"That I don't know," she said. "I can think of several people who might wish just that."

"Are you referring to Miriam's family?" I said, before I realized I shouldn't be making such statements to others who might not have the same reason to suspect them as we did. But then I realized that there was very little, if anything, that we knew about residents of the Home that Hannah Bissela didn't also know. And she probably knew it well before we did.

"Yes, there is them," she said. "But right here at the Home there are at least two residents I would suspect, if Pupik had not been caught with the gun in his hand."

Of course, Mrs. K and I were very interested in who else might have a motive. Mrs. K said, "And who would those people be? I wasn't aware Maria had made any enemies here."

Mrs. Bissela looked right and left before lowering her voice and saying, "It wasn't the enemies she made that were the problem, but the friends."

Mrs. K looked at me, and I just shrugged my shoulders. I had no idea what Mrs. Bissela meant.

Also in a low voice, Mrs. K said, "I'm not sure I understand, Hannah. What do you mean it wasn't the enemies but the friends?"

"Well," she said, "what I heard was that Maria was a flirt. And sometimes she went well beyond flirting."

Of course, we knew about her relationship with Pupik, and although as I said it usually was unlikely Mrs. Bissela would not know such a thing even before we did, the way we accidentally found out might mean only we were aware of it. So I didn't ask whether Pupik was one of people with whom Maria "went well beyond." Besides, he isn't technically a resident of the Home.

Mrs. K pursued the matter further. "You mean she had … she had relations with one of the residents?"

"All I know is that she was seen going into Albert Mitchell's apartment one evening when Albert's wife, Jenny, was away at her mother's."

I should explain that Albert is one of the caretakers at the Home, and he lives on the premises with his wife. The owners think there should always be someone there in case of emergencies, and at the time Albert was that someone after the other help went home at night.

"And so you think Albert might have become upset with her for breaking off their relationship and then Albert …"

"No, no," Mrs. Bissela said. "Nothing like that. No, it is Jenny, his wife, I would suspect. I understand she found out about Maria's 'visit' and made a terrible scene. I didn't hear the argument personally, but I'm told she used some very strong language, said what she would do to Maria if she ever caught her near Albert again, or something like that."

"Hmm, I see," Mrs. K said. "And do you know whether she, that is, Maria, ever did come near Albert again?"

Mrs. Bissela shook her head. "No, but I wouldn't be surprised if she did. Albert is a good-looking young man, and like I said, Maria liked to, mmm, spread herself around a bit."

That we already knew. I wondered whether perhaps she spread herself a little too far this last time.

Jenny Mitchell definitely had to go onto our list.

"You said at least two you could think of. Is there someone else you think disliked Maria enough to kill her?" Mrs. K asked. Clearly she wanted to take advantage of Mrs. Bissela's vast store of information while we had the chance.

"Well," Mrs. Bessela said slowly," there is Harvey Plotnik."

We were both surprised by this. Harvey Plotnik is at least seventy years old, looking his age, and not particularly wealthy, so neither of us could imagine why Maria would be interested in him.

"So why Harvey Plotnik?" Mrs. K asked. "He hardly seems a likely person."

"No, I suppose not. But as you know Plotnik fancies himself as quite the ladies' man."

"Yes, he does put on airs," Mrs. K said. And of course a person's self-image doesn't always match how other people see him. In many cases that's a good thing.

"He does. He thinks he is God's gift, as they say. So apparently he met Maria one day and she probably said something, or gave him a look, to make him think she fancied him. Probably how she looks at anyone wearing pants. But being Plotnik, instead of taking it for what it was, or wasn't, he had the *chutzpah* to ask Maria if she would like to, well, to spend some time with him, if you know what I mean."

"That did take *chutzpah*," I said. "At his age."

"It certainly did," Mrs. Bissela said. "And if Maria had simply said no thank you, that might have been the end of it. But that is not what she did."

"No?"

"No. What I heard is that she laughed in his face, and then she told the story around, making Plotnik seem like quite the *shmendrik*. Like a fool."

"Now that you mention it," I said, "I do seem to recall hearing about that, but I didn't pay much attention and never knew the details." Yes, it's a sin even to listen to gossip, but you can hardly go around with earplugs to avoid someone telling you something you shouldn't hear.

"Well, as a result," Mrs. Bissela said, "Plotnik called Maria some very nasty names, and I am told he threatened to get even with her. So as I said, I would not discount him as a suspect. If it had not been Pupik who killed Maria, that is."

"Yes, if it hadn't," Mrs. K said. And best left at that, I thought.

A few minutes later Mrs. Bissela left us, no doubt to put her ear to another door, and we were left to contemplate our list, which was growing longer by the minute.

****

"I suppose we should have a talk with each of them," Mrs. K said. "See if we can learn anything useful."

"Yes," I said, "and we might as well begin with Naomi. Perhaps we should now be telling her about Maria taking her mother to the casino. We never did, you know."

"That's true. And although Maria is no longer a … a problem for her, it might be a good idea for her to know that her mother just might have a gambling problem."

So Mrs. K telephoned Naomi and arranged that we

should meet with her the next day.

Non-Pupik suspect number one.

****

After lunch the next day—it must have been about two o'clock in the afternoon—Naomi knocked on Mrs. K's door. Mrs. K and I were enjoying a game of cribbage after lunch in her living room at the time. I opened the door to find a much different-looking woman than the one who had asked for Mrs. K's and my help, not that long ago. She no longer was looking worried and nervous. In fact, she looked quite contented.

"So, Naomi dear, your little problem seems to have solved itself in a most unexpected, and tragic, way," Mrs. K said.

"Yes, I suppose so," Naomi said. "But the bitch got what she deserved, so I won't pretend I'm sorry about it." She then quickly apologized for her language, but she didn't take back the sentiment.

I was a little surprised to hear Naomi's tone. It's true she was very concerned about how Maria might have been treating her mother, but I would have thought a little more compassion was called for.

Mrs. K obviously was displeased as well, because she said, "Surely you don't think anything Maria might have done with your mother warranted her being … being murdered."

To her credit, Naomi looked at least a little embarrassed. She said, "I'm sorry, I guess that wasn't very nice to say about someone who's died. It's just that she was such a … such a bad person, at least where my mother was concerned. And you know, I think mother was finally coming to see that, at least I'd like to think she was. But I guess it doesn't really matter now. I'm just glad Maria's gone. Though I'd rather she had just gone away, of course."

We nodded in agreement.

"And isn't it terrible about Mr. Pupik?" Naomi said. "I understand he was found holding the gun that killed her."

Mrs. K looked over at me. "Yes," she said, "several of us were there. He says he didn't do it."

Naomi laughed. "Yeah, sure. What would you expect him to say?"

Mrs. K didn't answer that, but asked, "Were you or your husband or brother there to see it too?"

"Us? Well, yes, we were all there, but we didn't go into the kitchen. Actually, my husband and I watched the play—you did a great job putting it on, by the way. Anyway, you asked me to come over. What did you want to see me about?"

"Well, for one thing," Mrs. K said, "I wanted to let you know what we found out about where Maria was taking your mother."

"What's that matter now? She won't be taking her there anymore."

"Yes, of course, but that doesn't mean there isn't still a problem."

"What problem?"

"Maria was taking your mother to a casino, where they gambled."

Naomi thought about this for a moment, then said, "Okay, but I don't really see how that's a problem. I guess we've all put a few nickels in the slot machines from time to time."

I refrained from mentioning that I and Mrs. K had not. Well, until the other day, at least. We were probably not typical when it came to casinos.

"Yes, but that isn't exactly the point," Mrs. K said. "If that's all it was, there's no reason to be concerned. But you told us there were large amounts missing from your mother's bank account, and it's possible this money was spent at the casino. Gambling can become a habit, an expensive one. We thought you should know, so you can watch for any indications your mother might have such a habit."

"Oh, I'm sure it was Maria's idea to go to a casino. Mom has never been a gambler or anything, at least as far as I know. Anyway, I'd appreciate it if you both would kind of drop the matter now that Maria is … is gone. And forget that I asked you to … to check up on her."

So now Naomi not only considered the whole matter closed, she wanted us to do the same. Maybe that was because Maria was now no longer a threat and she was embarrassed at how worried she had been.

Maybe. But in any case there was no use pursuing the matter further.

"I understand," Mrs. K said. And we left it at that.

****

We next knocked on Albert's door. There was no answer, but as we were turning away from the door, Albert's wife Jenny arrived. She seemed to be in a bad mood, and we could smell some kind of liquor.

I was uncertain what to say to her; we had planned to talk with Albert first, to find out if we could hear his side of the story Mrs. Bissela had told us. But here we were, so after we introduced ourselves—we had not actually met Jenny before, although we had seen her around—Mrs. K took the plunge:

"I guess you know about what happened in the kitchen during the Purim party," Mrs. K said. I'm sure she was hoping to see how Jenny would react to Maria's death. She saw.

"Yeah, I know, and that bitch got just what she deserved. Good riddance to bad rubbish, I say. So what about it?" The second person within the hour to use that term for Maria.

Jenny's tone was definitely hostile, and I thought to myself perhaps it would be best to leave now. But Mrs. K was not quite through.

"We were just trying to speak with anyone who was at the Purim party and might have seen exactly what happened—"

She didn't get any further with her question. "Look," Jenny said, interrupting Mrs. K, "Just because I was at the damn party doesn't mean I know anything more than you do. Everyone knows who shot the bitch, Pupik did. And I don't mind saying if I'd had the chance, I'd've done it too. Now if you'll excuse me, I've got better things to do than answer your stupid questions." And she shoved past us, opened the door, and slammed it shut.

Mrs. K and I just looked at each other for a moment, then she said, "Well, Ida, I guess we got our answers."

"Yes," I said, "sometimes it isn't even necessary to ask the questions."

****

That left Harvey Plotnik.

"I kind of like Plotnik," I said to Mrs. K as we walked down the hallway. "He's such a gentleman, even if he is a bit conceited. I can't believe he would do anything so terrible."

"Maybe so," Mrs. K said, "but sometimes you can push someone too far and they ... what is it ... go off the rails."

"I suppose so," I said. So we headed for Harvey Plotnik's apartment.

On the way, I said to Mrs. K, "I hate to admit it, but every time I hear the name Plotnik, I think of that joke from a few years ago about the diamond."

"I don't recall such a joke," Mrs. K said, "So *nu,* tell me already."

"It's the one where Sadie is admiring Zelda's beautiful diamond ring. 'Such a huge diamond,' Sadie says. 'Yes,' Zelda replies, 'it's the Plotnik diamond. But it comes with a curse.'

'A curse?' says Sadie? 'What is the curse?' And Zelda replies, 'Plotnik.'

Mrs. K was polite enough to laugh, but I'm sure she'd heard it before. I also assume Plotnik had, more than once.

****

As Harvey Plotnik was not in his apartment, we made our way to the lounge, to see if he was there. It was almost four o'clock, tea time, anyway, so most of the residents would be there, or at least come by for a cookie.

As we were waiting for tea to be served, one of the kitchen staff—it was the new girl, Betsy—wheeled out a cart with trays of delicious-looking cakes and cookies.

When she stopped by us, Mrs. K and I each reached for a cookie, Mrs. K one with raisins and me a chocolate chip. But before I could take mine, Betsy leaned over and said, "You might not like those, Mrs. Berkowitz. They're the, you know, the different ones."

I did know. Lately they had been adding baked

goods—bread, cookies—made without wheat—it is what they call "gluten free," although I'm not exactly certain just what a gluten is—at the suggestion of Dr. Menschyk. Apparently the wheat is not good for some people. Personally I don't care for them. Why is it that when something to eat is referred to as being "healthy," it almost never is also referred to as being "delicious"? Anyway, I took one with raisins.

Betsy moved on with the cart. Mrs. K watched her for a minute as she went from one group of residents to the next.

"What do you see?" I asked her.

She looked away and picked up her cup and half-eaten cookie. "Nothing, Ida," she said, "just … just Betsy. A *shaina maidel.* Nice looking."

Also very well endowed, as they say. No doubt that was why Little Wasserman was staring so intently at her *bristen* when she bent over to serve him his tea.

Chapter 20

We decided we had had enough with snooping for the present, and we would take a day off, so to speak. For at least a day there would be no interviews with residents, no *shmoosing* with the police—no Albert, no Plotnik—just a quiet day at the Home. All this investigating of murder and chasing after suspects—I don't know how policemen like Corcoran do it, but they can have it. Even Mr. Sherlock Holmes must take time off to play the violin occasionally.

So the next afternoon Mrs. K and I were playing bridge with Jacob Wasserman ("Big Wasserman") and Mrs. Bissela, thinking about bids and contracts instead of guns and suspects. It was a pleasure.

About a half hour into our game, Doris Lehmann approached the table where we were playing. Now Doris is a slightly-built lady somewhere in her eighties, and she is just a little *farblondzhet.* You know, her *challah* is braided a little too loosely. But such a nice person; everyone likes her. Doris seemed to be carrying something in her hands, which turned out to be a jar. A jar of pickles.

"I hope I'm not disturbing anything," she said, putting the jar down on the table in such a way it almost tipped over. Pickle juice, I'm sure, does nothing good for either the table or the carpet, and two of us grabbed the jar and steadied it.

"Not at all," Wasserman assured her, not to be unfriendly even if it did put quite an abrupt stop to our game. He is always so polite. "That's quite some jar of pickles you have there, Doris."

"Yes, isn't it?" Doris said. "They were just ready this morning, and I wanted to share them with everyone. I want you each to have one." She seemed quite proud of her pickles, and it is true I had heard she made an excellent kosher dill.

"I've brought some napkins from the dining room," Doris went on, and she passed one out to each of us.

Nu, one can hardly refuse a homemade pickle, and I have to admit it's one of my favorite foods, either accompanying a pastrami sandwich or by itself. So each of us accepted a large pickle, and Doris left us, saying, "Be sure to let me know how you liked them."

Each of us took a little nibble on a pickle. Each except for Mrs. Bissela, who did not.

I'd noticed out of the corner of my eye that Mrs. Bissela was looking a little peculiar—or maybe uneasy—while Doris was passing out the pickles. And as soon as Doris was out of earshot, I found out why.

"So tell me, Hannah, what is it with the pickles? You don't look anxious to try one. Don't they agree with you?"

"They wouldn't agree with you either if you knew where they came from," she said.

Now I was confused. "You mean Doris didn't make them herself? She bought them somewhere? Somewhere that wasn't kosher?" I wasn't actually sure whether Mrs. Bissela kept kosher, but what else could it be?

"No, no. Of course she made them. That's the problem."

"That she made them?" I was even more puzzled.

"Not, *that* she made them, but *where* she made them."

Still no light bulb is going on over my head, as they show in the comic pages. I looked at Mrs. K, and she just shrugged, so I wasn't alone in not understanding.

"Hannah, please come to the point," Mrs. K finally said. "Where exactly did Doris make these pickles?"

Mrs. K has a way of asking a question that usually receives an answer, and this was no exception.

"In the toilet."

I laughed. "You know," I said, "I could swear I heard you say she made them in the toilet."

But Mrs. Bissela was not laughing; she was instead nodding.

And suddenly I felt the need to sit down. Which was strange, because I was already sitting. There was silence all around.

Mrs. K, who was now looking quite concerned, was the first to speak up. "Hannah, would you mind explaining what you mean? She made these pickles while she was in the toilet? On the toilet? Surely not!"

Mrs. Bissela looked uncomfortable, which is for her somewhat unusual, as she generally delights in telling whoever will listen the gossip she has picked up.

"Well, Hannah?" Mrs. K prompted.

"It's like this," Mrs. Bissela said. She was looking quite miserable. "One of the ladies who cleans our rooms—I think it was the one called Marjorie—told old Mrs. Moskovitz that when she had gone into Doris' bathroom to clean it, she had discovered that Doris had been making pickles in the …" She seemed unable to finish her sentence.

Mrs. K finished it for her. "In the toilet?"

Mrs. Bissela just nodded once or twice. Then she burst out with a rapid explanation, as if a dam holding back the words had burst. This, at least, was the Mrs. Bissela we knew.

"I saw you had all had a *nosh* on the pickles, and I didn't want to upset you, and then I thought I should have said something right away, before you took a bite, but then it was too late."

"*Nu,* Hannah," Mrs. K said, surprisingly calm under the circumstances, "just tell us about the toilet."

"Yes. Well, the cleaning person told Mrs. Moskovitz that she asked Doris about it and Doris said whatever she usually used broke and she didn't have anywhere else to make her pickles and the toilet was just the perfect size and, well, that's what she used."

"In the toilet bowl? *Oy gevalt!*" I was starting to feel quite ill at the thought.

"No, no, not in the toilet bowl. In the toilet tank. You know, where the water is stored that you flush with."

I looked at Mrs. K, who looked at Wasserman, who looked like I felt. But at least it was not as bad as it could have been.

Mrs. K didn't seem disturbed, so much as angry.

"So we are *noshing* on pickles that were made in a toilet tank?"

Mrs. Bissela, looking a bit sheepish, nodded.

"And was this reported to the management? Did either you or Mrs. Moskovitz tell someone in charge about it?"

"I … that is, we … no."

"I see."

"We didn't want to hurt Doris' feelings. You saw

how proud she is of her homemade pickles."

"And if she was proud of her homemade bombs, would you not tell someone she was making them?"

"Well ... yes ..."

"Of course. Now this is not as serious as maybe a bomb, but as you can see, it's quite upsetting to those who only find out about it too late." She looked at me and at Wasserman. "I think it would be best if someone reported this, and before too many more of those pickles are *fressed.*"

With that, Mrs. K stood up and walked out of the lounge. I stayed where I was, looking down at the nibbled-on pickle that now looked to me like it was a large caterpillar that had expired on my plate. Wasserman did the same, while Mrs. Bissela just sat there looking miserable. And she hadn't even eaten a pickle.

And that was how Mrs. K found us when she returned several minutes later. And rather than looking concerned, as when she had left, she was looking quite pleased with herself.

"*Nu*, so I found Mrs. Rothstein—you know, the woman who has taken Pupik's place for now—and I told her about Doris and the pickles."

"And she was shocked?" Wasserman said.

"On the contrary. She laughed."

"Laughed?"

"Yes, because this Marjorie, the cleaning person, she reported what she had found to her boss, who reported it to the management, which was at that time still Pupik. Well, you can imagine what happened then."

"Pupik told her to stop doing it?" Wasserman said.

"Yes, to put it mildly, and I imagine he threw in a

threat to evict her from the Home, if not have her drawn and quartered. Anyway, she promised not to do it again, and to pay for any damage to the plumbing she might have caused."

This was, of course, very good news, and I immediately felt much better.

But then I had a further thought: "But what about the pickles we just ate? What about that big jar she was carrying?"

Mrs. K smiled and sat back down at her place at the table. "Pupik made her throw them out, the ones from the toilet" she said. "And then he apparently did something that will surprise you like it surprised me."

"What?" I said. "He took away her toilet privileges?"

Mrs. K laughed at that. "No. He admitted to her that he had tried her pickles and quite liked them, and that the Home would buy her a proper container so she could continue to make them without either plugging up the plumbing or poisoning the residents."

At that we all just stared at each other in astonishment. A second time Pupik has spent the Home's money when he didn't have to.

And at least for that moment, I didn't feel so bad that Mrs. K and I had promised to help Pupik prove his innocence.

A man who likes kosher pickles can't be all bad.

Chapter 21

The next day Mrs. K and I were ready to resume our snooping.

After breakfast, we retired to the lounge and Mrs. K got out her familiar note pad. "It's time," she said, "that we try to narrow down our list of suspects and zero in, as they say, on one or two. As we did before, we should start with the assumption that Pupik is not guilty. That he didn't shoot Maria."

"But it is very difficult to ignore what we know we saw," I said.

"Yes, but just for purposes of our investigation, we must ask ourselves, if Pupik didn't kill her, and I realize that's a big 'if,' then someone else did. So who could that someone be?"

I had to agree with her on that. Who indeed.

"And as every detective from Mr. Sherlock Holmes to Hercule Poirot will tell you, we must look for a motive and an opportunity. We have talked already about those who might have the motive—Miriam's family, Maria's husband, Jenny, Plotnik, and so forth—but we haven't really considered which of these people had the opportunity to do the act. If we now consider opportunity, perhaps we can narrow down the suspects. Do you agree?"

"That certainly sounds right. No matter how good a motive someone might've had to kill Maria, if they were not at the Home when she was killed, or they were seen somewhere other than the kitchen at the time, we can cross them off the list. Unless of course they hired someone to do it for them."

"Yes, of course. But I think we can safely put that possibility aside for the moment and concentrate on those who might have pulled the trigger. We'll assume whoever wanted to kill Maria did so themselves."

I nodded. I wasn't seriously suggesting they hired someone, you understand. But we have to consider all possibilities.

"So logically," she continued, "it had to be someone who not only was at the Purim program, but entered the kitchen. And was wearing a costume, according to Miriam. They might not have been there long, just long enough to shoot the gun and leave. Is that not so?"

"Yes, of course," I said. "And we already know that Naomi and her husband and brother were at the program. Most of the others, like Maria's husband, we don't know. How should we be finding out? Ask them?"

"Yes, we can ask them when we have a chance. But I had something else in mind first. I think we should have a talk with some of the people who were working there, find out what they might have seen."

"You mean the servers and such? Yes, that does seem like a good idea. Do you know who they were?"

"Not all of them, but I do remember seeing a couple of the regular staff. We can start with them."

****

So at lunch Mrs. K and I looked around the dining room to see if we remembered any of the staff serving that day having been working at the Purim program.

"I see Frank Nelson over there," I whispered to Mrs.

K. "It seems I remember him being one of the servers at Purim."

"Yes, I think you're right," Mrs. K whispered back. "We shall have a talk with him right after lunch."

Frank had been working at the Home for a long time. He had had some personal problems in the past when his wife was very sick, and then they had a baby and were in need of money … but I think that all got worked out satisfactorily, because lately he had seemed quite happy. A new child will do that for you.

Mrs. K and I waited to approach Frank until most of the residents had left the dining room and the wait staff was cleaning up.

"So, Frank," Mrs. K said as he turned and saw us, "how is the family? Everyone is well, I hope?"

Frank smiled and said, "Yes, everyone's just fine, thanks."

"And you're enjoying being a father, I assume?"

"Absolutely. It's really changed both of our lives. Mine and my wife's, I mean."

"Wonderful," Mrs. K said. "Ida and I had a small question to ask you, if you don't mind."

"A question? About what?"

"Actually, it's about the Purim program. You were one of the servers there, weren't you?"

"Well, we weren't actually doing a lot of serving, just the *hamantaschen* and coffee and such, but yes, I was working there. Why do you ask?"

I expected Mrs. K to make up some reason that didn't involve Maria's murder, but instead she came right out with the truth.

"I'll tell you honestly, Frank, but please don't tell anyone else. You of course know about the tragic thing that happened that day."

"Of course. Who could forget? It's still hard to believe something like that happened here at the Home. And that Mr. Pupik should have been the one who did it … I mean, it's all just so weird."

"Yes, weird does seem to describe it. But it turns out some aspects of it are not as … as clear as they might seem, and we're trying to learn the truth."

Frank looked at us and smiled like you might smile when you are sharing a secret with someone. "I get it," he said, bringing his voice down. "You're playing detectives, just like those other times. And I understand you were a big help to the police. Is that what you're doing now?"

"In a way," Mrs. K said, sounding a bit uncomfortable. "Let's just say someone has asked us to help. Can we ask you a few questions?"

Again the secret-sharing smile from Frank, like we're conspirators together.

"Sure," Frank said. "Ask away."

"Thank you. First, do you remember seeing anyone at the program who you didn't recognize, or at least who you were surprised to see?"

"You mean, like if some dude from off the street had wandered in?"

"Well, yes, I suppose. Anyone you don't remember seeing here before. A stranger."

"Hmm. To tell the truth, because of the play you guys put on and all that, there were lots of people there I didn't recognize. Like kids and grandkids of the residents. And maybe some invited their friends. And besides, most people were in some kind of costume or wearing a mask, so they weren't recognizable."

Of course, this was true, and unfortunately, we couldn't ask Frank about specific persons, like Maria's husband or Miriam's family, without making it seem like we suspected them. Which we did, of course, but we couldn't tell Frank that. So Mrs. K tried another approach.

"Yes," she said, "I understand. So let me ask this: Can you think of anyone—any adult, I mean, other than a resident—who you did recognize?"

Frank closed his eyes and seemed to be thinking very hard.

"Well," he finally said, "I can think of a few, if it's any help. There was Mr. Schultz, the man who owns the deli where we get our meats and cheeses. He was there with his wife and kids. He was wearing a mask over his eyes—you know, like the Lone Ranger?—but he was easy to recognize."

Mrs. K took out her note pad and a pencil and made a note, but I'm sure we were not to be suspecting Mr. Schultz. Or his wife and children.

"And there was Mrs. … Mrs. Warner, I think her name is, who sometimes helps with the gardening." Mrs. K dutifully made a note.

Frank gave us several more names of people we had no reason to suspect, although one never knows what might turn out to be important later.

"That's about all I can remember," Frank said, and then he seemed to think of something. "Except for that I-talian guy, you know, Mrs. Cartwright's friend."

No, we didn't know. But Mrs. K certainly wished to find out.

"You don't know his name, this friend of Mrs. Cartwright?" she said. "You don't mean her husband,

John, do you?"

Frank laughed. "No, I know who John is. I mean, he works here, doesn't he? In fact, he was at the Purim thing, now that I think of it. Said thanks when I brought him some coffee, and I recognized his voice behind the mask." Mrs. K made a note, this time with good reason.

"No, this is the guy who came to pick her up one time and sort of wandered in here and asked if I knew where she—where Mrs. Cartwright, that is—might be. He looked sort of I-talian, if you know what I mean. Tall, dark, shiny black hair combed back. Good-looking dude. I said I didn't know where she was and he kind of wandered out again. Then a few days later I saw him as I was leaving after work. He was picking Mrs. Cartwright up. At least she was getting into his car. I remember it because he was driving this real fancy car–a Jaguar–and I really love those cars."

Mrs. K scribbled a note. "And he was at the Purim program?" she asked.

"Yeah, I'm pretty sure I saw him there. He wasn't in a costume or anything, just kind of wandering around, like he was looking for someone."

"Thank you, Frank. That's very helpful," Mrs. K said. "So I have just one other question."

"No problem. Shoot."

Not the best choice of expressions under the circumstances, but Mrs. K didn't seem to notice.

"Can you remember," she said, "if you saw anyone—a resident, a member of their family, anyone—go into the kitchen in the few minutes before … well, before we discovered what had happened there?"

Frank again closed his eyes and appeared to be thinking very hard. When he opened them, he was

146

shaking his head slowly.

"No, I can't," he said. "At least no one I recognized. I mean, I definitely saw a couple of people go into the kitchen at one time or another, but they were wearing costumes and masks, so I don't know who they were. And around the time you mean, I was actually watching the play. I'm sorry I can't help you there."

Mrs. K made a quick note, and then she smiled at Frank and said, "But you've been a big help, Frank. Ida and I really appreciate it."

"Hey, I'm glad to help. It was a terrible thing, what happened to Mrs. Cartwright. I guess old Pupik went off his nut or something. Anyway, at least they know who did it. And to be honest, you folks will be better off without Pupik, from what I hear."

And unfortunately, what Frank said was hard to deny.

"Yes," said Mrs. K, "I guess we'll have to wait and see how this all comes out. Thank you again, Frank. And now we'd better let you get back to work."

"No problem. But you're right. I've got a few tables to clear before the setup for dinner. See you around."

And with that Frank went back to work, and Mrs. K and I went back to the lounge, to process this new information.

New, and possibly changing the game.

Chapter 22

"So we've added another person to our list," Mrs. K said when we had seated ourselves comfortably.

"Yes," I said, "except this person we don't know his name. Just that he looks Italian and drives a fancy car, which isn't much help."

"Oh, I don't know about that," Mrs. K said. "I'm sure other people at the Home will have seen this man around, and perhaps someone will know who he is. The important thing is that he apparently is—or was—a friend of Maria's, and he was looking for someone, probably her, at the Purim program. But there is another significance to learning about this man."

"Oh? What's that?"

"Well, I've been wondering something about what I overheard in Pupik's office. You'll recall he was arguing with a woman, and he told her she couldn't just 'walk away' from him. So why was she doing that? Why was she 'walking away'?"

I thought about this. "Didn't she say something about him not keeping his promises?"

"Yes, I think so. And we don't know what those promises might have been. So if Pupik was breaking his promises to Maria, that is, if it was his fault she was 'walking away,' it would seem she would be more angry at him than he at her, and it would not be as likely a motive to kill her. But if what caused the argument was something bad she did, we would expect Pupik to react angrily, as he did."

I was not sure I was following Mrs. K's reasoning. "So you're saying that to get Pupik as angry as he sounded, and perhaps angry enough to kill Maria, she had to have done something to provoke the breakup?"

"Yes, exactly. And now we may have learned what that something was."

"That she was cheating on both her husband and Pupik, with this Italian-looking fellow?"

"Well, don't you think this is a possibility?"

Actually, I did think so, now that Mrs. K mentioned it. And to be honest, I was quite pleased with myself for having followed her reasoning this far. It's not always the case.

"So much for finding evidence to help Pupik," I said. "We seem to have found more evidence he's guilty, or at least more of a motive for killing her."

"Yes," Mrs. K said, shaking her head a bit, "jealousy must be right up there with money as a common reason people kill each other. But it's not all bad for Pupik."

"No?"

"No, because now that we know about this Italian—we keep calling him that, but he probably will turn out to be Armenian or Norwegian or something—now that we know about him, we have another person who is not Pupik and who might have killed Maria."

"And who was apparently looking for her just before she was killed," I added. "Yes, it's a mixed bag for Pupik, as you say."

And I wasn't sure whether we had made some progress, or just created a further *mishmash.*

****

149

We didn't discuss Maria or Pupik or anything so unpleasant for the rest of the day. *Nu,* a person can only take so much thinking about murder and adultery at one time. We played a game of bridge, read the newspaper, and discussed the latest political scandals, of which there is never a shortage.

But the next morning, Mrs. K said, "Ida, I was thinking that yesterday we were supposed to be narrowing down our list of suspects. But instead we seem to keep adding more to our list, including at least one we didn't even know existed before yesterday. At this rate, we'll soon have everyone except us on the list."

"So how do we begin taking people off the list? And with whom should we begin?" I asked.

"I think I would begin with John, Maria's husband. He seems to me to have had the best motive, if we don't count Pupik, and if for the moment we assume he knew about Maria's affair with Pupik."

"A better motive than Naomi and her family?"

"Yes, in the sense that, at least in this case, I believe jealousy is a more likely motive for murder than either money or concern for a parent's welfare," Mrs. K said. "Think about it. What emotion does each motive cause in a person?"

I thought about that for a minute. "*Nu,*" I said at last, "a person who kills for money would be driven by greed, wouldn't he? By wanting more than he has?"

"Yes," Mrs. K said, "I would agree. And concern for a parent?"

"I suppose the emotion there would be love, wanting to protect someone you love. But it would depend on what you are protecting them from, wouldn't it? I mean, if their life were in danger that would be much different than if it was something else that needed protecting."

"Exactly what I'm thinking," Mrs. K said, which I admit surprised me a *bissel,* as I don't often think exactly as well as she does. Perhaps with all these investigations we're having, something is rubbing off on me. "And which are we dealing with here, with Miriam's family?" Mrs. K asked.

"Well, certainly there was no reason to think Maria was endangering Miriam's life. Just her money, or perhaps other property that the family wanted for themselves."

"Yes. And that leaves jealousy," Mrs. K said.

"I see what you mean," I said. "Yes, I agree a jealous husband or lover is more likely to kill someone than a concerned daughter."

"At least we can start with the husband and jealousy," Mrs. K said. "And then work our way through other motives."

"But you already 'interviewed' John Cartwright, didn't you? When you went to him for a massage?"

"I suppose I did, but we know more now than we did then. He was not really what you would call a suspect then."

"So you will be going back for another massage?" I asked.

"No," she said, "you will."

"Me? Why me? Mr. Sherlock Holmes I'm not. And I'm sure he wouldn't send Dr. Watson out to investigate for him."

"Actually, he might. But in any case, it must be you," Mrs. K said, sounding quite certain about it, "because he'll be suspicious if I go back and ask the same kind of questions I asked before."

"But what would I say to him? What would I ask?"

"You can act like someone who knows nothing about him, so you can ask about his family, commiserate with him about his loss. See how he reacts, how really sorry he is she's gone. You know. You're very clever, Ida, and I'm sure you'll get just as much information as I would."

I appreciated the compliment, and I wish I could say I felt confident it was justified, but I can't. There was only one thing I saw myself getting out of a session with John Cartwright.

And that was a massage.

Chapter 23

We inquired at the desk to find out whether John Cartwright would be making his regular visits to the Home, considering the recent tragedy of his wife's murder. I admit neither Mrs. K nor I was particularly surprised to learn that he had cancelled only one day's sessions, immediately after Maria's death, and otherwise it apparently would be business as usual. So I made an appointment for the next time Cartwright would be at the Home, which it turned out was the next morning.

When I entered the little room that Cartwright uses on the ground floor of the Home, I was surprised at how empty it seemed: just a long table—the one with the bagel at one end that Mrs. K had described—one chair, and a screen, and there was also a small desk in the corner, the kind where a big flap folds down to expose the shelves inside and to make a writing surface.

Our suspect was not there yet, so I looked around, just in case there might be a clue somewhere. But there was almost nothing else in the room, and in the desk just what looked like an appointment book. On the desk was a small picture frame turned face down. I went closer to see better the picture, which was on the back of the desk. It turned out to be a photograph of three people hugging each other and smiling into the camera. It was Maria and her husband on either side of someone else I didn't recognize, a tall man, good-looking, all smiling and seeming very friendly. In fact, the man just fit the description Frank had given us of the "I-talian-looking" man who had been looking for Maria. Whoever he was, he was either *mishpocheh*, family, or at least on very good terms with them both. Not so likely either a lover or a killer, which I'd have to tell Mrs. K

But as I was peeking at the picture, Cartwright opened the door. He surprised me and I jumped back a bit—I don't know why, except maybe because I was looking at something I wasn't supposed to see—and although he didn't say anything, his face had the same look my mother's used to get when she caught me with my hand in the cookie jar.

With what seemed to be some effort, Cartwright's face changed to a more welcoming expression. He introduced himself and I did the same.

From Mrs. K's earlier description of her appointment, and the fact that I had in the past had what they call massage therapy for various minor conditions, I was more or less prepared for what it was to get a massage from Mr. Cartwright. What I was not prepared for was what came with the massage.

Cartwright left the room so I could undress and get under the sheet lying across the massage table. Like Mrs. K, I got undressed only to my underwear. Believe me, this wasn't as easy as it sounds. I'm not used to taking my clothes off in a strange room in which there will momentarily be a strange man, even behind a screen. But this was for the investigation and not for pleasure, so I did what I had to.

Cartwright knocked on the door and asked if I was ready, and when I said I was, he entered. He asked me what type of massage I wanted—to treat some problem or just to relax. I said just to relax.

"Then you want a Swedish massage," he said. I actually didn't care what country it came from, but I said that was fine.

I'll be honest: Although I was quite tense when Cartwright began, what with the reason I was there and my reservations about being undressed, once he began with the touching and the squeezing I found it quite pleasant. In fact, I was becoming so relaxed, I almost fell asleep.

But suddenly I remembered why I was there, and what I was supposed to find out. I was there to snoop, not to snooze!

Between squeezes and pushes I said, "Maria was your wife, was she not? I'm sorry for your loss."

"Yes, thank you," he replied. Then he went back to squeezing and pushing.

So what should I ask next? Mrs. K would have known just the right questions, but she was not there, so I had to think quickly, not my strongest quality.

"It must have been quite a shock, what happened," I said.

There was a long pause before he answered simply, "Yes."

I decided to be a little more direct. I asked, "Did your wife and Pupik know each other very well?" As soon as I asked the question, the squeezing suddenly became less like a massage and more like making orange juice.

"Ouch! Not so hard, please," I said.

He said, "Sorry," but not like he meant it. This man, I thought, doesn't like Pupik (for which he is hardly unique, as I've said), or maybe doesn't like how well

Pupik knew Maria.

I tried a different approach. "Why do you think a man like Pupik would do such a thing?"

These were not, of course, questions I would ordinarily have asked a grieving man whose wife had recently been murdered, but I wanted to hear his reaction.

Oy, did I hear it.

This time he stopped what he was doing and stepped toward where my face was and said, in a less than friendly tone, "You're a friend of that nosey Mrs. Kaplan, aren't you?"

"Well, yes, I ..."

"I thought so," he said, sounding very angry. "As I recall, she asked a lot of questions about me and Maria too. Well, from now on you and she'd better keep your noses out of my business, if you know what's good for you."

It was like I was in the middle of one of those movies where the tough guys are always threatening what they'll do to the other tough guys. And nine times out of ten they actually do it! I would've gotten off the table and left the room as fast as I could, except I wasn't wearing anything except my underwear. So I just stayed where I was and waited to see what happened.

Fortunately, no one was bumped off, as they say, in particular me. I nodded that I understood.

And believe me, I did.

Then he turned around and headed for the door, saying, "I guess our session is over. No charge." But before he reached the door, he stopped and walked quickly back to the desk in the corner that I had been snooping in. He lifted the flap in front to close it, turned a little key that was in the lock, put the key in his pocket, and this time he left and closed the door behind him.

I just lay there for several minutes to get myself calmed down, because all of his threatening, and with me in such a vulnerable position, had made my heart pound as if I'd just climbed two flights of stairs. When I felt better, I got up and quickly went behind the screen and got dressed, in case he should change his mind and decide to come back and bump me off.

As soon as I had buttoned the last button, I quickly left the little room and walked as fast as I could back to my apartment. I put on the kettle and when the water boiled, I made myself a strong cup of tea.

With *schnapps*!

Chapter 24

When I was feeling better and none of my parts was shaking, I called Mrs. K and asked her to come over.

"Is something wrong, Ida?" she said on the phone. "You sound worried."

"Worried? No, more like scared. Or at least I was, but I'm better now."

"Did you go to see John Cartwright?" she asked. "You had an appointment this morning, didn't you?"

"*Oy,* that's exactly what scared me. But I'll explain when you're here."

"I'm coming," she said. "As soon as I find my shoes. I'm sure I put them somewhere…"

She hung up. It's not only shoes I'm often looking for. It's keys, glasses, whatever gets far enough away from me so I can't see it. As we get older, it seems our belongings find more and more ways to hide from us. It's like a game, for them at least.

So Mrs. K arrived about five minutes later. Apparently her shoes were hiding behind the sofa, where she had taken them off because her feet were swollen. But you don't want a detailed report, I'm sure.

"So what happened, Ida?" she asked when she had taken a seat on my sofa. "What's this about being scared?"

I told her my experience with the massage, repeating as best I could remember exactly what Cartwright said.

Very quiet was Mrs. K while I told her about Cartwright's threat. And when I had finished, she was still quiet, thinking it over, I assume. She looked worried.

Finally, Mrs. K looked up and said, "Ida, that man sounds dangerous. It might be time to talk with Inspector Corcoran again."

That sounded good to me. This case was beginning to make me just a *bissel* nervous. Another person murdered we didn't need.

Especially if I might be that person.

****

Unfortunately, talking with Inspector Corcoran turned out to be not so simple.

That is, talking with him was no trouble. Mrs. K telephoned the police department—I was listening on the other phone—and reached the inspector easily enough. But before she could tell him about John Cartwright, he gave her some very bad news, at least for us.

"Before you go on, Mrs. Kaplan," he said, "I should tell you that I've assigned the Maria Cartwright case to Sergeant Porter. Although there are, of course, still some outstanding issues to resolve, it seems to be a pretty straightforward matter."

"Maybe not as straightforward as you think," Mrs. K said.

Corcoran laughed. "Perhaps, but when the spurned ex-lover of a married woman is found standing over her body holding the gun that killed her, which also just happens to be his gun, well, they just don't come much more straightforward than that. So it seemed to me a good opportunity for Sergeant Porter, who hasn't had a lot of experience with such cases, to gain some. I hope you understand."

There was silence on the phone. Neither Mrs. K nor I knew what to say to that. It's not up to us who the police put in charge of their cases. But still …

"But Inspector," Mrs. K finally said, "there are … are developments that you really should know about …"

"I'm sure you can convey them to Sergeant Porter and she will take them into account. Here, let me transfer you to her office. And as usual, Mrs. Kaplan—and you, too, Mrs. Berkowitz—I appreciate your assistance." And we heard a few clicks, and another phone rang.

Before I had a chance to wonder how Corcoran knew I was on the line—maybe that's why he's such a good detective—the bland voice of Sergeant Porter answered the phone.

"Porter here."

Where else should she be?

"Sergeant Porter, this is Rose Kaplan. You'll recall we met you when you accompanied Inspector Corcoran at the Julius and Rebecca Cohen Home."

There was a pause. Perhaps she was flipping through the pages of her memory, trying to find Mrs. K. Finally, she said, "Oh, yes. What can I do for you?" But it sounded more like, "What do you want?" with the emphasis on the "you."

"We wondered if we might come to your office and tell you about some new developments in the case that Inspector Corcoran said we should tell you about."

"What new developments?" Porter said.

"It would be easier to explain in person," Mrs. K said.

"Look," Porter said, sounding impatient, "I appreciate your wanting to help and all that, but I really haven't got time to listen to your theories of the case."

"No, you don't understand," Mrs. K said. "I haven't got a theory, just …"

But Porter cut her off. She was polite but sounded cold, like a plucked chicken.

"I really don't think there's much to add to the Cartwright case, is there? Suspect as good as caught in the act. But if Corcoran said you should tell me your so-called new developments, you'd better go ahead. I haven't got all afternoon."

Mrs. K hesitated, but then she cleared her throat and told Porter what we had learned, including how we had found out about the unknown man who seemed to be looking for Maria at the Purim carnival, and the way Maria's husband had threatened us.

When Mrs. K was through, there was a long silence at the other end of the line. I thought maybe Porter had hung up on us, but she hadn't. Gone to sleep, maybe. She finally said, "I see. A mysterious stranger, and a bereaved husband who didn't like you snooping into his affairs. That certainly ought to exonerate our suspect, Mr. … [I heard the rustling of papers] Mr. Pupik."

I know Mrs. K hates sarcasm, and no one likes to be talked down to like that. I could see her face becoming quite pink, but she "kept her cool," as my son would say, and answered, "We just thought you should know these things. Everything is not always as it appears."

"Yes, I'll keep that in mind. And now I really haven't any more time for this. Thank you for the information. Goodbye."

And that was that. There was no longer a Porter at one end of the line, and two very angry ladies there were at the other.

161

Mark Reutlinger

Chapter 25

After our most unpleasant telephone conversation with Sergeant Porter, Mrs. K and I sat with our own thoughts. I'm sure our thoughts were pretty much the same, though.

After a minute or so, I asked Mrs. K, "So do you think we should give up with the looking into who killed Maria? I mean if the police don't want us to…"

"But Ida," Mrs. K said, "it's not for the police that we're doing the snooping, as you put it. It's for Pupik, because we said we would. And even if he's not at all a nice person, we've given our word. And besides, Margaret is a very nice person, and you can see how she's suffering from what Pupik did. Or did not do. You know what I mean."

This was true, and I had to agree with Mrs. K. We owed it to Margaret to do our best for her husband, even if no one else seemed to want to.

****

And it turned out her husband was going to be at the very center of the rest of our day. You'll recall how surprised Mrs. K and I were to receive a call from Margaret, Pupik's wife, saying Pupik wanted to see us. Well, we were even more surprised when Mrs. K received a telephone call from Pupik himself.

Mrs. K had gone back to her apartment while I took a little snooze, still recovering from my "relaxing" massage. About 11:30 I got up and, after washing my face with cold water and changing clothes, I made my way to Mrs. K's apartment, so we could go together to lunch, as usual. When I entered, Mrs. K was just hanging up the phone. She had a strange look on her face.

"Who was that on the phone?" I asked.

"You'll never guess," she said. That somehow sounded familiar. "So I'll tell you. It was Pupik."

"Pupik? Not Margaret this time?"

"Yes, the man himself. And he sounded quite distraught."

"Well, we know why that is, of course, being suspected of murder."

"No, it's different. Remember when we went to see him, he was subdued and worried; but this time he sounded almost desperate."

"So *nu,* what did he say?"

"He wants to speak with us again. But not at his house this time."

"No? So where does he want we should talk?"

"He said anywhere we wanted, except here at the Home, of course. He suggested we meet for lunch somewhere."

"For lunch? I don't understand."

"I don't either, except he was very anxious that we meet and talk. I of course couldn't refuse, so I suggested the Garden Gate Café, since it's where we usually eat when we're downtown."

"And he agreed?"

"He did. I said we could meet him for lunch tomorrow, but he said he would rather it be today, so I agreed. We're supposed to meet him at 12:30."

I was totally confused. Why meet with us again so

soon after we talked at his house? Why at somewhere other than his house? And why so urgent it had to be today?

I supposed we would find out soon enough.

****

Just before noon, Mrs. K and I asked the Home's receptionist to call us a taxi. The shuttle was running again, but it would not leave in time for us to meet with Pupik at 12:30. While we waited, we went over what could this meeting possibly be about.

"Perhaps Pupik has decided he doesn't want us becoming involved in his case after all," I suggested. "We were surprised he asked us in the first place."

"Yes, but then why not just say so over the phone? And if for some reason he wanted to tell us in person, why not at his home, where he asked us to help? And why the hurry?"

"Too many whys. And you said he sounded distraught. Something must have happened since we saw him. Perhaps something to do with the police."

And before we could ask ourselves any more questions, the taxi arrived and we gave the driver where we wanted to go.

The answers would no doubt come soon.

****

The taxi dropped us off right in front of the Garden Gate Café. Usually when we're downtown shopping, we go there for tea and maybe a bagel with a *shmeer* or a bran muffin. For lunch not so often. It was crowded, and noisier than we were used to.

We looked around but didn't see Pupik anywhere, so we found a table for four in the corner where it was less noisy and sat down. We both sat on the same side, next to each other, so we could talk with Pupik across the table when he came. We were just looking at the menus our server had brought us when I heard, "Good afternoon, ladies." I looked up and Pupik had sort of appeared out of nowhere. Perhaps he came in the back way?

"Good afternoon," we both said. Mrs. K added, "Please sit down."

He sat. He didn't look well, again like he hadn't been sleeping. Who could blame him? But at least now we would find out what this meeting was all about.

"Have you ladies ordered yet?" he asked.

We said we hadn't, and he signaled to the server to come over. When she did, he told us to go ahead and order. I ordered a tuna salad sandwich and a cup of jasmine tea. Mrs. K ordered just a green salad and peppermint tea. (When we're out, we like to drink something more interesting than our usual.) Pupik ordered just a cup of coffee. I guess he wasn't hungry.

We soon found out why.

Once the server had left our table, Pupik said, "I'll come right to the point, ladies. I really appreciate your offering to help me prove I didn't kill Maria Cartwright. Even if it turns out there's nothing you can do to help, I appreciate your trying. But now a new problem has come up, and I need your help even more."

Needless to say, we were all ears. What could he be talking about?

"The reason I wanted to meet with you here," Pupik continued, "was that what I have to say I couldn't say in front of Margaret, as you'll see."

Here he paused and seemed to be gathering his strength to go on. He swallowed hard, like someone about to jump into a cold swimming pool, and, well, plunged in.

"But first," he said, "I must have your solemn promise that you'll tell no one what I'm about to tell you. That it will go no farther than this table."

Mrs. K and I looked at each other in puzzlement, but we both nodded our heads. "Yes, if it's what you want," Mrs. K said, "we won't tell anyone else. So what already is this all about?

Another pause and deep breath.

"I know this will be a shock to you, but I had been … I had been having an affair with Maria Cartwright."

Gottenu! Mrs. K and I almost fainted. It was the last thing either of us expected Pupik to say, at least to us. And immediately we had to decide, independently and without a chance to talk it over, how to react. My mind was racing: Should we tell him we already knew, or at least strongly suspected? Or should we pretend this is something completely new to us? And if we pretend it's a total surprise, how should we react? As usual, I decided to take my cue from Mrs. K. I waited to see what she did.

Always quick on the uptake, Mrs. K took just enough time to make a decision. She then cleared her throat and said, "You mean, you and Maria had been … had been seeing each other? At the time she was killed?"

He nodded. "Yes. I know it was a mistake, and it was terribly unfair to Margaret, but like they say, there's no fool like an old fool. And that's just what I've been. And to make things worse, at least with regard to the murder, we had just had a falling out. We had argued, and, well, we said some terrible things to each other."

"I see," Mrs. K said. "And you are telling us this why?"

Why indeed. A few days before, we were the best of enemies. Now we were Pupik's confidants. How quickly today's goat becomes tomorrow's lamb.

Pupik put his head in his hands and did not speak for a moment, then he looked up and said, "I haven't told you the whole story yet. I was hoping, of course, that our … our relationship would not come out. That somehow I would prove I was innocent without anyone—and especially poor Margaret—ever finding out …"

So Margaret did not know, or at least she hadn't told Pupik she knew.

"… But then … then…"

He paused and took a deep breath before continuing.

"Then I received this." He took a folded piece of paper from his pocket. But before he could do anything further, our lunches arrived. He put the paper back in his pocket.

"Go ahead and have your lunch," he said. It's probably better I wait for what I next have to say until after."

Oy, that didn't sound promising. Eat now before you lose your appetite?

But we did eat, and the tuna salad was delicious. Mrs. K's green salad looked nice too, and with many fewer calories than what I was eating.

As we ate, I could not help glancing at that pocket where Pupik had put back the paper. Curiosity made me eat faster so we would find out what was on it sooner. I only hoped I would avoid the indigestion.

After we had finished and were sipping our tea, Pupik again took out the folded paper and handed it to Mrs. K. She unfolded it and read aloud, in a low voice:

"Dear Mr. Pupik: I know about you and Maria

Cartwright. I'm sure your wife and the police would also like to know. If you want me to keep quiet, scare up $10,000 cash in one week. I'll contact you then and tell you how to get it to me. And remember that if you try to trap me some way, I'll make the whole sordid story public. It's up to you.

"[signed] A friend."

Some friend! Mrs. K passed the letter to me. It was written in a very uneven hand, as if the writer were trying to disguise their handwriting, which in this case would seem likely. Either that or they just had terrible handwriting. The paper was ragged at the top where it apparently was torn off a pad carelessly.

I handed the letter back to Mrs. K, who refolded it and handed it back to Pupik. And then we all just sat there for at least a minute, with nothing to say.

Talk about *tsures*! This man has more troubles than Noah had animals.

But at least one thing was clear: Mrs. K's hearing is just fine, and despite what Inspector Corcoran said about the possibility she was mistaken, it was indeed Maria's voice she heard that day. It's not often she's wrong, as I should know very well.

Finally, Mrs. K asked Pupik, "Have you told the police about this?" But as soon as she said it, she (and I) realized it was a silly question. Nevertheless, Pupik answered it:

"No, I can't do that, don't you see? I would be telling them about the affair with Maria, which will be all they need to hang me. And it would probably end my marriage to Margaret, which is the last thing I want now. As I said, I've been hoping I could prove my innocence before the police found out about ... about us."

Okay, here was another dilemma, which were becoming like the candles on my last birthday cake: much too many. Mrs. K and I had already told Corcoran about the affair, or at least that we suspected it. And although Corcoran quite correctly pointed out that Mrs. K might have been mistaken about who she heard arguing with Pupik, they already had enough information to investigate further and, no doubt, eventually find out the truth even if we hadn't mentioned it. In fact, our short talk with the Porter woman seemed to indicate just that. So should we tell Pupik the police already know? That would mean telling him we already knew, and that we told the police. Then if he was either convicted of murder or his marriage was ruined, or both, he would consider us the reason. And in a way, we would be.

Oy gevalt! My head was beginning to spin like a *grogger*.

Mrs. K, who as I've said thinks much faster than I do, took what you might call a neutral position. She said, "It's true it would be better for you that the police don't know about this … this affair between you and Maria. But have you considered that they might already know, or if not they will find out once they begin their investigation in earnest? So maybe it is just as well to tell them yourself."

But Pupik was having none of that suggestion. "Absolutely not," he said. "If they find out, they find out. I can't stop them. But I'm not going to help them, either. Not unless and until I can prove my innocence."

Mrs. K sighed. "So what is it you want from us?"

"Well, I was hoping you might see if you could find out who could possibly know about … about me and

Maria. I've thought and thought about it, and I can't imagine who it might be." He paused and took out a handkerchief from his pocket and wiped his forehead. He was *shvitzing* like it was July, but it was only April. He put the handkerchief back and continued: "But then I'm not thinking too well right now. Anyway, I know you have your … your sources at the Home …"

Sources he wants? The only source I can think of is the *yenta* Hannah Bissela. What she doesn't know about who's doing what to whom is not worth knowing. But we already decided she probably didn't know, and certainly she wouldn't be blackmailing Pupik. Would she?

Pupik waited for an answer. Finally, Mrs. K spoke up. "I don't know that we'll be able to find out who wrote that letter, but we'll try. Whether or not you're responsible for what happened to poor Maria—and Ida and I are trying to stay open-minded on that since our previous discussion—and in spite of this terrible thing you've told us about your … your relationship with her, it's not right for someone to try to take advantage and threaten you that way. If we find out who wrote that letter, we'll tell you. But I still advise you to tell the police. As I said, they'll find out in time anyway."

"I've told you I can't," Pupik said, shaking his head, but then he added, "but I know you are giving me good advice. I know I don't deserve your help, and I really do appreciate your offering it."

Just then the check came, and Pupik took it and handed a credit card to the server. On any other day, I would have thought I was dreaming: The man who spends money like every dime was his last, picking up the check for my and Mrs. K's lunch. But as I've said, this was not any other day.

Maybe the *momzer* was becoming a *mensch*.

****

We thanked Pupik for lunch and prepared to leave, when Mrs. K thought of something important.

"Perhaps," she said, "I should take a copy of that letter, just in case the handwriting gives us any clue. You never can tell."

"Of course," Pupik said. "I saw a drugstore down the street. Let's go in there and see if they have a copy machine."

So we left the Garden Gate Café together, just like old friends. The drug store did have a copy machine, and Pupik made a copy of the letter for us to take with us. Then he thanked us again, said goodbye, and walked off.

From the look on his face and the tone of his voice, he clearly was relieved to have finally told someone his dark secret, someone he hoped could help him.

What I hoped was that we hadn't just given the man false hope.

And ourselves a big pain in the *tuchis!*

Chapter 26

On the way back to the Home, we took a bus, just for a change. It takes longer, but it gets us out among ordinary people. You can imagine that no matter how pleasant and friendly are the residents of the Home (and believe me, they aren't always either one), we are all, as they say, of advanced years. Let's face it: Most are, if you'll excuse the expression, *alter cockers*. Old farts, I guess you would say. Whereas on the bus, there are people of every age, some happy and some sad, some talking and some listening to music with a *dingus* in their ear, some reading a newspaper, some just sitting and staring straight ahead. It's refreshing.

We found two seats together but didn't discuss what Pupik had said. It was going to take some time for us to digest all these new facts, as well as those we already knew and had already told the police, but now had sworn not to reveal. In a way, we were supposed to be helping the police, and at the same time we were also supposed to be helping their chief suspect. They say in Yiddish, *Mit eyn tokhes ken men nit tantsn af tsvey khasenes.*

You can't dance at two weddings with one *tuchis*.

****

Back at the Home, both Mrs. K and I felt as though we'd been through a wringer. (You remember when washing machines had wringers? No? Ask your grandmother.) First the man we said we would help to prove his innocence tells us a secret—which it happens we already knew, but had to pretend we didn't—that makes it highly likely he isn't innocent at all. Then he tells us another secret—by this one we were surprised for real—that only complicates matters.

At least the tuna salad was good.

"Ida," Mrs. K said as we sat in the lounge (well clear of Mrs. Bissela's antenna), we have now two distinct problems—Pupik's guilt or innocence, and the attempt to blackmail him. But I can't help feeling that they're in some way related."

"What do you mean, related?"

"I'm not sure. But as Mr. Sherlock Holmes learned on more than one occasion, the kind of people who deal in blackmail may also deal in even greater crimes to achieve their ends."

"So which of these matters should we focus our attention on first?" I asked. At which wedding should we dance?

"Let us start with the blackmail letter, only because there's a more immediate need. Pupik has only a few days to decide what to do."

"Fine," I said. "So where do we begin?"

"The logical thing," Mrs. K said, "is to ask ourselves who might've known about the affair between Pupik and Maria."

"*Nu,* we knew, didn't we? So anyone might have."

"Yes, but the way we found out—my overhearing their argument—it isn't likely anyone else would also find out. It required the office being empty because Hilda was away, and Pupik and Maria arguing loud enough for me to hear just as I was near the door. No, the fact we knew says almost nothing about who else might have known."

I had to agree. "So maybe Maria told a friend or relative about it," I said.

Mrs. K thought that over for a minute, then said, "Of course that's possible. And if she did, there's no way for us to know who she told, so we might as well not try. But again it seems unlikely. I mean, if you were having a secret affair with someone that could ruin your career if it were to come out, would you tell anyone about it?"

Now that question was not so easy to answer. First of all, I could not imagine myself having such an affair, cheating on my sweet husband David, may he rest in peace. And even if I had, I certainly wouldn't have told my friends about it. Okay, maybe I would tell Mrs. K, but I'm sure she would never try to blackmail me about it.

Apparently Mrs. K didn't really expect an answer to that question, and she continued: "Who, then, is the most likely person to learn that a man is cheating on his wife?"

I thought about this for a minute, and then I saw where Mrs. K was going. "I suppose his wife."

"Yes, that's what I think. She might overhear a conversation with his lover, or find a note from her carelessly left out, or someone she knows might see them together and tell her. There are a million ways."

"You're now suggesting that Margaret found out about her husband and Maria, and Margaret is trying to blackmail him? You can't be—"

"No, no, Ida. It's the other way around. Just as a wife would be a logical person to learn of her husband's cheating, so a husband would be a logical person to learn his wife was cheating on him."

Suddenly I saw where Mrs. K was going with this.

"So you're suspecting Maria's husband, John?"

"I won't go so far as to say I suspect him, just that he's the logical person to start with. He might have found out his wife was cheating with Pupik, and he decided to turn it to his own advantage, so to speak."

"Well, Rose, if he has a guilty conscience, that might explain why he was so upset about my asking questions of him. But remember, you had that massage from him before Maria was killed. Looking back now, what do you think? Might he have known about Pupik?"

"Yes, it's possible. Remember, I told you how he seemed not to trust her, seemed to think she might be doing to him what she had done to her previous husbands. And one thing I didn't mention to you at the time, because it didn't seem important, was about Pupik himself."

"Oh? And what was that?"

"He spent several minutes complaining about how Pupik was trying to take advantage of him, always asking for a bigger percentage of what we pay him, threatening not to let him continue with his business at the Home. Said Pupik was—how did he put it?—always 'putting the squeeze on him.' No, he doesn't care for Pupik at all.

"I'm sure he would be only too happy to squeeze Pupik for a change."

****

Just then, Jacob Wasserman ("Big Wasserman") wandered over in our direction, picked up a magazine, and sat down across from us, giving us a polite nod and a smile. Of course, we couldn't continue to discuss Pupik's problem with Wasserman so close by, even if his hearing is not so wonderful these days. We changed the subject to the latest news about the recent Israeli elections, and waited for Jacob to leave.

Leave he did not, however. In fact, he put down the magazine and closed his eyes. He was either asleep or doing a fine imitation of it. Since we couldn't be sure, after about ten minutes, we decided if Jacob was staying, we would have to leave. Which we did.

We adjourned to my apartment, and after settling down in the living room, we took up the conversation where we had left off.

"So how do we find out whether in fact Maria's husband knew she was cheating on him with Pupik?" I asked Mrs. K.

"Hmm. Perhaps I need another massage from the husband," Mrs. K said.

I wasn't so sure. "What, you'll ask him if he knew about his wife's affair? Remember how he warned me that we should not snoop into his business. He would not exactly welcome you back. Besides, you already learned he was suspicious of Maria and didn't like Pupik. Do you think he'll tell you why?"

"Not exactly. You'll recall I asked Pupik to give me a copy of the blackmail letter."

"Yes. I was wondering what you would do with it. I mean, what it said was pretty easy to remember. And the way it was written, it seemed to be in a disguised writing, so even if we were handwriting experts, which of course we're not, we couldn't tell who wrote it."

"Perhaps you're right. Still, I have an idea that might possibly be helpful …" She seemed to drift off into thought. Then she said, with that determined look she can get, "Yes, I'm going to give it a try."

I assumed she would tell me in due time what it was she was going to try.

And whether or not it succeeded.

Chapter 27

I had a hair appointment the next morning, so I didn't see Mrs. K until lunchtime. As soon as lunch was finished, Mrs. K picked up the cup with her unfinished tea, took me by the arm and steered me to an empty corner of the lounge. She did stop long enough for me to go back for my own tea, but she obviously had something she was anxious to tell me. In fact, she looked like she couldn't wait to tell me, which I have to say is unusual for her. Mrs. K generally is a very patient person. We sat down on a sofa and from her pocket she took out two pieces of paper.

I saw that she was holding the blackmail note Pupik had copied for her and also another piece of paper I didn't recognize.

"Does this have something to do with the blackmail note?" I asked her.

"It does. Do you know where I was this morning?"

"No, should I?"

"Well, no. But you recall I said the other day I might have another massage from John Cartwright?"

"Yes, and I recall saying I didn't think he would say anything more useful than he already did. I take it that's where you were this morning?"

"I was. And you were right—he didn't tell me anything more than I already knew. In fact, as you predicted, he wasn't too happy to see me, and I was careful not to ask any nosey questions. He of course couldn't refuse to give a resident, even me, a massage and keep his business here at the Home."

"*Nu,* so why are you so excited?"

"Well, it seemed to me the best clue we have to who sent the blackmail note is the note itself. In fact, it's the only clue."

This seemed logical, but not helpful.

"But how will the note help us, as it's printed in a disguised handwriting?" I asked.

"You know, Ida, Mr. Sherlock Holmes was a great believer in handwriting analysis. In fact, he was able to tell many characteristics about a person from their handwriting, such as whether the writer was a man or a woman, their age, even whether two writers were related. I believe he wrote a monograph on the subject."

"But again, this handwriting was disguised."

"Ah, but I did a little reading about this at the library yesterday, and it turns out even attempts to disguise one's handwriting, unless by someone who is themselves an expert, sometimes fail, because certain characteristics remain without the writer realizing it. An expert, then, given a sample of the known handwriting of the person, often can determine whether the known and the questioned writing are by the same person."

This was news to me, but it seemed still not to solve our problem. Or rather Pupik's problem.

"That's all very well," I said, "but a sample of Cartwright's actual handwriting we don't have, and neither do we have a handwriting expert to look at them."

I thought that would surely end this line of discussion, but Mrs. K only looked more pleased with herself. She held up the other piece of paper that had been in her pocket and waved it in the air.

"That's where you're wrong, Ida," she said. She seemed to be having a bit of fun with telling me this, and I was happy to go along with it.

"Okay, so what is it on that piece of paper that's so important?" I asked.

"Well, I wanted to get a sample of Cartwright's handwriting, and I thought of a way. While he was giving me a massage, I told him how wonderful I felt after the last time, and how I'd like to have massages more regularly, but can't always make it on the days he comes to the Home. I asked him whether he works somewhere else where I might see him. He said yes, he has a room in a fitness center downtown. So I then asked would he write down the address for me, and to be sure to put the name of the fitness center and the days he's there on it, because I have a terrible memory at my age and might forget these things."

"And that's what's on that piece of paper?"

"It is." And she showed it to me.

I was impressed. "That was clever of you," I said. "But suppose he'd just given you a business card with the address on it?"

Mrs. K smiled and patted me on the knee. "That's a good question, and to tell the truth I hadn't thought of it. But I suppose I would have said I can't read the small print and please write it out large on a piece of paper."

Of course. Mrs. K is never at a loss for an idea.

"So that takes care of the sample," I said. "But we still don't have the handwriting expert."

"Yes, and that's a harder problem," she said.

"But I just may have an answer for that, too."

No wonder Mrs. K looked so pleased with herself. I

couldn't wait to hear how we would become handwriting experts.

"So will we take a quick course in whatever they call handwriting detecting?"

"I think it's called graphology. But no, nothing that drastic. My thought is that we'll hire a handwriting expert to tell us if the two papers match.

"But wouldn't it be easier, and much cheaper, if we could get someone to do it for free?" I said.

"And just who is this 'someone' you have in mind?"

"Well, you know how Isaac Taubman's policeman son, Benjamin, helped us out in the past."

"Yes, but he is no . . . oh, I see. You mean that Isaac should ask Benjamin to have someone at the police department—their handwriting expert—look at these two papers and give us an opinion?"

"Isn't it worth a try? He has helped us before."

Did I mention that Taubman is more than just someone who sits at our table at meals? He's very fond of Mrs. K, and in fact they've gone on what I would definitely call "dates," although I'm sure Mrs. K would insist they were just keeping each other company at the symphony or the movies. There are lots of ways to tell when a woman is sweet on a man, and Mrs. K has all the signs. When she's going out with Taubman, she wears her best dresses, puts on a little lipstick and makeup, and uses a dab or two of her favorite perfume. Not like when she's going out with me or other lady residents, and of course I wouldn't expect anything else. I remember how it felt to go out with my David when we were courting. And although we cannot be expected to feel like we were twenty-five again, fifty years doesn't put out the fire; it just damps it down a bit to a warm glow.

So Mrs. K and Taubman are, in my granddaughter's words, a "thing." How much of a thing, or how hot a thing, I am not certain, but a thing for sure.

Mrs. K seemed to think over my suggestion, but she shook her head.

"I don't think we can ask for such a favor," she said. "I felt uncomfortable the last time we did, and here we would be asking Isaac to ask Benjamin to ask some expert at the police department who we don't even know . . . . No, I think we will have to get our own expert."

"And just where do you plan to find such a person?"

"Oh, I'm sure they're around. Like when a man hires a detective to find out who wrote the love note to his wife, that sort of thing."

"Okay, let's suppose we find someone. Who's going to pay for this expert? They're probably very expensive, like lawyers. I assume you didn't intend that we should ourselves spend the money."

"Of course we won't pay. I'd expect Pupik to pay, if he wants to find out who wrote that note."

That sounded a lot better. I couldn't imagine Pupik refusing to pay under the circumstances.

"So now all we have to do is find an expert. How do you propose to do that?"

She laughed. "Well, you're the computer whiz around here. Go find one."

It's true. Mrs. K may be a whiz at playing detective, and she has a really logical mind so she can follow a clue to its, well, its logical conclusion better than anyone. But when it comes to computers, logic can only take you so far. It's like trying to speak a foreign language you never learned.

Here at the Home we have computer classes every

week, and for some reason I really enjoy them and have learned enough to use a computer to find out things I could never find out any other way. Mrs. K, on the other hand, insists she "can't be bothered" with the classes, but I think it's just that she has so many other interests she hasn't the patience to learn the computer language. *Nu,* no one can be good at everything, not even Mrs. K.

So of course I went down the hall to the Home's computer room—it used to be our Arts and Crafts room, but that's now down in the basement—and turned to the *maven* of all knowledge, Mr. Google. And under "Handwriting Experts" I found several names, not just local but all across the country. Of course, we could send the papers by mail anywhere we wanted, but I chose a local person, telephoned for an appointment, and reported back to Mrs. K.

"We have an appointment tomorrow at ten with a gentleman who sounds like he knows a thing or two about handwriting," I said. I also told Mrs. K what he charges. She didn't faint, but it's a good thing she knew we weren't paying for it.

Just then I thought of something I should have thought of earlier.

"Wait a minute," I said. "We'll have to show this fellow both notes, and we promised Pupik not to reveal his secret to anyone."

Mrs. K took some time to consider this little glitch. Finally she said, "That's a good point, Ida. And to tell the truth, I hadn't considered that we'd be revealing Pupik's secret, which he particularly didn't want us to do. Of course, we wouldn't be revealing it to anyone involved in the matter, or who knows Pupik."

"That's probably so," I said, "but I think I'd still be

a bit nervous about it. What if by some chance this person happens to know Pupik, or Maria? I mean, it's highly unlikely, but …"

Mrs. K nodded and appeared to be mulling this over. She looked carefully at the blackmail note again, putting her hand over one part, then another. She then looked up and said, "You know, Ida, I think we can get around your objection—that is, our promise to Pupik."

"How's that?"

"Well, look here." She put the note on her lap. "If we make a copy of the note and cover over or black out these names," indicating Pupik's and Maria Cartwright's names, "there really is no way to identify who this note was written to, or who it's about. It's just a note threatening to reveal someone's affair with someone else to his wife and the police. And on the sample I got from Cartwright, I think we can delete enough of the information so there's nothing identifying him, but still enough words to make a good sample."

I looked carefully at the two notes, reading them over without the names and other words Mrs. K had indicated. Something about it still bothered me.

"Yes, you're right," I said, "but what about the part about telling the police? If someone is threatening to tell another person's wife he's cheating on her, that makes perfect sense. But why would he also threaten to tell the police? That would mean the person having the affair is somehow in trouble with the police, or would be if his affair were revealed to them. Might that not make someone who has read the newspaper reports about the murder—and I'm sure there were stories about it in all the papers the day after it happened—put two and two together and come out with Pupik?"

Mrs. K laughed. "I'm not sure of the arithmetic, Ida, and while I think you're being a bit too cautious, I must admit I didn't think of that possibility. So just to be extra careful, we can also delete the words "and the police." After all, we only need some writing to compare to the sample I got from Cartwright; it doesn't matter what the writing says."

Yes, occasionally Dr. Watson thinks of something Sherlock missed

****

There wasn't much more we could do about the matter of the blackmail note until we saw the handwriting expert, so we took the rest of the day off from detecting. Mrs. K went to the library to return some books, and I caught up with some correspondence. Then I spent a half hour in our exercise room, on one of those machines that looks like a torture device but is really supposed to help you feel better. I think just still being able to do the exercises at all makes people like me feel better. It keeps us from thinking about how old we're getting. What do they say now? "Age is just a number." Well, maybe it's not that simple, but as my mother was fond of saying, *Az me vil nit vern alt, zol men zikh yingerheyt oyfhengern*: "If you don't want to grow old, hang yourself when you're young."

Chapter 28

So the next day promptly at ten in the morning Mrs. K and I knocked on the fourth-floor door of "Peter Brown and Associates, Forensic Consultants," on 82nd Avenue, not far from the Garden Gate Café, where we met with Pupik and he told us about the blackmail note. As I mentioned, I had found Mr. Brown's website on the computer. It stated that he had been "trained in graphology as an FBI agent for thirty years" before retiring. That seemed to me to be pretty good credentials.

The door was opened by a short, stout, balding man of about sixty. He smiled and said, "You must be Mrs. Kaplan and Mrs. Berkowitz. Won't you come in? I'm Peter Brown."

He stepped aside and we entered a smallish office, comfortably furnished with an antique-looking desk and high-back chair behind it, two smaller chairs with wine-colored upholstery in front of the desk, and an art-deco floor lamp that gave off a warm glow. A modern desk lamp shed bright light on Brown's workspace. It all looked very comfortable (although if Mr. Brown indeed had "associates," I couldn't see where they would sit).

We seated ourselves in the smaller chairs and Mr. Brown took his seat behind the desk. He folded his hands in front of him and said in a quiet voice, "I understand you have a document you want authenticated."

"Yes, that's right," Mrs. K said. She took the two

sheets of paper out of her purse and placed them on the desk. "What we need is a comparison of these two papers. We believe they were written by the same person. I saw him write this one," pointing to the address Mrs. K had Cartwright write, "but with regard to this one," pointing to the blackmail note, "we only suspect that it was written by him, and whoever wrote it apparently attempted to disguise his handwriting. We're hoping you can tell us whether the two were written by the same person."

Mr. Brown reached over and slid the papers to his side of the desk. He studied them for a minute before looking up and saying, "I see. This is obviously a very serious matter. Has it been referred to the police? They of course employ skilled handwriting analysts."

"No," Mrs. K said, "there are reasons we cannot involve the police, at least not at this time. That's why we've come to you."

Mr. Brown furrowed his eyebrows and seemed to be deciding how to proceed. After again looking over the two papers, he said, "Well, I don't see why I can't help you, or at least try. But I assume you realize that attempting to match an exemplar, that is, a known handwriting, to one that has been disguised is no simple matter, and it certainly cannot always be accomplished. That means, among other things—and to be perfectly frank—the analysis can be time-consuming and therefore more expensive than when the handwriting hasn't been disguised. And yet it might not yield a result either way, positive or negative. Is that acceptable to you?"

Mrs. K had already spoken with Pupik and explained our plans, and she had received assurance that we would be reimbursed for whatever it might cost to find out who sent the blackmail note. "Just have him send you the bill and pass it along to me," he had said. It occurred to me that Mrs. K probably didn't ask Pupik directly whether it was okay to spend his money even for no result, but I assumed that was implied. At least I hoped it was.

So Mrs. K answered yes, it was acceptable. Mr. Brown then pushed the papers away a little, sat back in his chair, folded his hands in his lap, and said, "Let me explain a bit about the process. There are twenty-one distinguishing characteristics an examiner might look for in a person's handwriting in order to compare a questioned document with a known exemplar. When both are written in an ordinary manner, comparing them is pretty straightforward. But when one has been deliberately disguised, it becomes more problematic."

"But you can still make the comparison?" Mrs. K asked.

"Not always. It may depend, for example, on whether this was the first time the writer tried to disguise his handwriting or whether he'd practiced and done it many times. Or it might depend whether he was at leisure or in a hurry when he did it, or mentally sound or disturbed. In other words, some disguised handwriting is much easier to detect than others. Until I examine your samples closely, I won't know which it is."

"We understand," Mrs. K said. "So when do you think you'll be able to get back to us?"

"Oh, I'd say in two or three days. I'm not particularly busy right now, but I do have one or two other projects that must take priority. Is that acceptable?"

"Yes, certainly," Mrs. K said. "Thank you."

We shook hands with Mr. Brown and left his office.

"Well," I said as we took the elevator back to street level, "that's about all we can do, leave it in the hands of an expert."

"I suppose so," Mrs. K said. "Meanwhile we should get back to the little problem of who killed Maria."

Oh yes, that little problem.

Blackmail. Murder. *Gottenu!*

Chapter 29

As it happened, it was the blackmail that continued to get our attention, not the murder.

The next afternoon, Mrs. K answered the phone and had a short conversation, during which she appeared to be hearing good news. She was a bit excited when she hung up the phone and told me who had called.

"That was Peter Brown, the handwriting examiner," she said, her hand still on the receiver. "He said after we left, he found himself so intrigued by the challenge of the disguised handwriting we had left him that he got to work on it immediately, and he's ready to give us his opinion. He asked us to come by this afternoon."

"So did he say what his opinion was?" I asked. "You seemed to be pleased by what you heard."

"No, he didn't exactly say what he'd found, but from his tone of voice I gathered it was good news. I hope I'm right."

I hoped so too. If Brown couldn't say the papers matched, I had no idea where we went from there regarding the blackmail threat.

So right after lunch Mrs. K and I returned to Brown's downtown office, and by 1:30 we were again sitting in front of his desk.

After the usual formalities, Mr. Brown looked at us both, smiled, and said, "I'm sure you folks want to know the bottom line before the details," to which we both nodded enthusiastically.

Still smiling in a grandfatherly way, although we were at least ten years older than him, he said, "Well, I believe we have a match. Not for absolutely certain, mind you, but a sufficiently high probability that my opinion would most likely stand up in court, should your, uh, matter come to that."

Mrs. K and I looked at each other and we both let out a sigh of relief. That was certainly good news.

"Would you like me to explain what I found?" Brown asked.

"Yes, certainly," Mrs. K said. "I find this whole process fascinating, and I'd love to hear how you came to your conclusion. And I'm sure Ida would also." She looked at me and I nodded.

So Mr. Brown proceeded to explain the process he followed and why he believed the two samples were written by the same person. I will not try to tell you everything he said here, even if I understood it all, which I didn't. But in a nutshell, he closely examined the disguised handwriting on the blackmail note to see which letters appeared to have been changed. Apparently someone trying to disguise their handwriting, especially for the first time, generally will not try to make every letter different from their usual way of writing it, but only certain ones. One way to tell which those are is to see if any letters are different from one word to another. For example, if the writer tries to change all his "a's," it's unlikely he will change them exactly the same in every word, since this is the first time he has tried to write them that way; whereas in his usual hand all his "a's" will be virtually identical, because he has written them so many times in his life. By eliminating all those disguised letters, the examiner is left with a close approximation of the writer's usual writing style. And even if he has tried to make them very large or angular or such, his usual pattern will emerge to the trained eye, when that eye is also looking at an undisguised example.

I don't know if that's clear, but the result was that there were more than enough matches between the two documents for Brown to believe strongly they were written by the same person.

And I hoped that was enough for us.

****

"So do you think what Mr. Brown told us is sufficient for our purposes?" I asked Mrs. K when we had returned to the Home.

"Yes, I think it is," she said, "because we already have good reason to suspect John is the blackmailer, and this just confirms it."

"*Nu,* so where do we go from here? To Corcoran? To Pupik?"

Mrs. K thought about this for a moment, although I'm sure she had been thinking about it well before this.

"It's an interesting question, Ida. I don't believe we can go to the police—that is, back to the police—because they'll of course insist on seeing the whole letter and knowing to whom it was written, and we promised Pupik we wouldn't do that."

"And do we tell Pupik?"

"Yes, eventually. But while that would satisfy his curiosity, it wouldn't solve his problem to know who sent the letter. We want to tell him he doesn't have to worry about paying anyone to keep quiet. So I have a better idea."

I wasn't surprised. "And what is that?"

"I will write to John Cartwright."

Now I was confused. "You'll write? How will that help?"

"Think about it, Ida. Cartwright knows he's committing a crime. He's counting on Pupik not knowing who he is, and in any case not going to the police. Suppose he receives a letter, anonymous like his was, saying something like, 'I know about the blackmail letter and I have proof you sent it. If you don't write another note to Pupik saying to forget about your demand—if you try to carry out your blackmail scheme—I shall turn you in to the police. Unlike Pupik, there's nothing stopping me from doing so.' Do you think he'll still try to collect from Pupik?"

I thought about this for a moment. "No," I said, "I'd think not. He doesn't know who you are–I assume you will disguise your handwriting better than he did," at which Mrs. K laughed, "so he would be taking a big chance on getting arrested. But of course as you just said, we can't go to the police because of our promise."

"Of course, but Cartwright doesn't know this, does he? So we won't have to tell anyone else, including the police."

"That is quite ingenious," I said. "It puts Cartwright in a position he can't squeeze out of."

"I hope so," Mrs. K said. "I shall write the note tomorrow. And then we can tell Pupik what we've done. He should be quite relieved."

"Relieved and grateful, I would think."

So it appeared we had solved The Case of the Anonymous Letter, although we still had work to do on The Case of the Murdered Maria.

I was sure we would be getting back to that shortly.

Chapter 30

It was the next afternoon, a sunny day, and Mrs. K and I joined some of the other residents in a trip to the park. It was good to relax and get away from thoughts of murder and blackmail, and we returned from the park refreshed and with everyone in a good mood.

It didn't last long.

"Something is clearly on your mind," I said to Mrs. K. She was looking very thoughtful. "Is it about the murder investigation?"

She sighed. "Yes, of course. Something you said when we were talking about your brother Max."

"About Max? What did I say?"

"You pointed out that we don't really know what people are like just from their appearance or how they act in public. I wonder whether we've taken that into account."

I wasn't sure what Mrs. K was getting at, but I gave it a try. "You mean that perhaps we need to think differently about Pupik? Perhaps we've been misjudging him all these years, when he's seemed to be such a *momzer*, and he's been a *mensch* all along?" There was, after all, the incident with the pickles.

Mrs. K laughed. "Well, that's not exactly what I had in mind. But now that you mention it, I do think we need to talk with him again. There's a very important question we have failed to ask."

This time we didn't travel out to Pupik's house to talk with him, but we telephoned him from my apartment. Mrs. K dialed the phone in the living room and I listened in on the extension in the bathroom. I always feel a little silly using a phone in the bathroom, sitting on the toilet lid, but that's where it was installed before I arrived at the Home, and that's where it still is. I just have to be careful not to drop the receiver in the bathtub. It has almost happened more than once. Better than pickles in the toilet, but still …

Margaret answered the phone, and after a few words of polite conversation, Mrs. K asked if we could speak with her husband.

"Of course," Margaret said. "But I should warn you he's feeling particularly depressed today. They've set a trial date, and the police still seem quite convinced he's guilty. Even our lawyer doesn't sound very hopeful."

It was more than a minute before Pupik finally came onto the line. He sounded definitely confused and bewildered by what was happening in his life. Who can blame him? Being accused of murder will put a twist in anyone's *gatkes.*

"Mr. Pupik, I have to ask you an important question," Mrs. K began.

"I'll try to answer if I can," he said. "But first, have you made any progress with my … my case? Are you any closer to finding out who killed Maria? Or that other matter we discussed?" He said the last thing in a softer voice.

"Maybe a little closer on the first matter," Mrs. K said. "I think things are becoming a *bissel* clearer. I hope after we talk they'll be clearer yet. On the other matter, I think we have eliminated the problem, about which we can talk later."

I could almost hear the sigh of relief on the other end of the line. In a much more cheerful voice, Pupik asked, "What do you want to know?"

"Surely you've asked yourself, if Maria was shot with your gun, and you didn't shoot her, how did the person who killed her get hold of your gun?"

"Yes, of course I've thought about that, wracked my brain for an answer, but I can't … I just can't think straight these days. I've been so nervous and upset …"

"I understand," Mrs. K said in her most soothing voice. "So let us go over it together." It was hard to believe she was talking this way to Pupik, who used to talk to her—to everyone—in such an abrupt manner. But life brings unexpected changes.

"Where did you last remember having that gun?" Mrs. K asked.

"I do remember that," Pupik said. "As you may know, I'm a bit of a gun collector, and that particular pistol was part of my collection. It was—is—beautifully engraved, and it has a custom-made holster decorated with several semi-precious jewels."

"You mean it was just for display, and not for shooting?" Mrs. K asked.

"No, it was quite serviceable," Pupik said. "I sometimes used it for target practice. I like to use a variety of firearms—that's part of the interest in collecting them—and that was a particularly accurate pistol. From the early 20th Century." Talking about his collection, Pupik sounded more like himself than when talking—or thinking, I'm sure—about his dilemma.

"So where did you have it last? On your wall at home?"

"No. As it happens, I had brought it to the office one day a few weeks before the … the incident, meaning to take it to a local gun shop to be repaired."

"You mean it didn't work?"

"No, it worked, but the trigger was a bit loose, so sometimes it was difficult to pull it, and sometimes just the opposite, it fired too easily."

"You mean it had—what do they call it—a hair trigger?" I asked.

"Yes, that's what it's sometimes called. Anyway, it was something I couldn't fix myself, so I was taking it to an expert."

"I see," Mrs. K said. "And so you took it to this … this expert?"

"Well, no. I got very busy that day and also the next day, so I put it away in a drawer and then I kind of forgot about it. Then maybe a week later, I remembered I had meant to take it in to the gun shop, but again I was too busy to get away. So I asked Hilda if she wouldn't mind taking it to the shop for me when she was going in that direction. The shop is all the way across town, you see."

"And did she do that? Take it to the shop?"

"To be honest, I don't know. She said she'd be glad to take it, but it would have to wait until she was going out that way. I said I was in no hurry, and to please just put it aside and take it whenever she had the chance. I saw her put it on a shelf in her office, but now I can't recall whether it was still there the last time … when I was last in her office."

There was a long pause while both Mrs. K and I thought about what Pupik had said. If he was telling the truth, and I think for our purposes we had to assume he was, either that gun was taken from the shop where Hilda brought it, which seems unlikely, or the person who shot Maria must have taken it from Hilda's office. Even I could put that two and two together.

Suddenly I remembered something from when we were in Pupik's office that day Mrs. K overheard the argument with Maria, so I put my two cents into the conversation.

"Tell me," I said, "was the gun you left in Hilda's office in any kind of … of container?"

"Well, yes," Pupik said after thinking for a few seconds. "I think I had put it into an old shoe box, having nothing else to put it in."

"Well, then it was still in your office when … when …"

"When what?" Mrs. K and Pupik said together.

I decided there was no use beating this bush around any longer. "When we were in Hilda's office the day … the day …" I could not come right out and say "the day you had an argument with Maria in your office."

Fortunately, Mrs. K rescued me. "I know what day Ida is referring to," she said. "It was about two weeks before Purim. We, ah, didn't get around to seeing you as we had to leave unexpectedly." This was Mrs. K doing a fine tap dance around the delicate issue, and it seemed to be succeeding, as Pupik didn't ask for details. "So why, Ida, do you say it was still in Hilda's office then?"

"Because I saw such a shoe box on a shelf. I didn't think anything of it at the time, of course, but now …"

"Yes, now it's more significant," Mrs. K said. "So, Mr. Pupik, you now should think hard as to who came to see you—who was in Hilda's office, but Hilda wasn't there, so no one came to see her—who came to see you during the time between the Tuesday two weeks before

Purim and the Purim party.

"Because there's a good chance one of them took the pistol from that shoe box and shot Maria with it."

****

There was a long pause again. Finally Pupik said, his voice unsteady, "I … I can't remember. I don't get a lot of people coming to see me each day, other than my staff, and I hardly think any of them even knew Maria—Mrs. Cartwright, that is. But I will think about it and send you a list of whoever I can recall."

"One other thing," Mrs. K said. "Did you tell the police what you just told us? I mean, about where the gun was?"

"Yes, I think so, at least in general terms. I remember they asked me, 'If it was your gun, and you didn't use it, how did someone else get hold of it,' or words to that effect." I told them I didn't know, and explained briefly about leaving it in Hilda's office. But I don't think they believed me."

And that was the end of the conversation. Mrs. K thanked Pupik. I hung up the phone in the bathroom and went to the living room to talk with Mrs. K.

"So do you really think someone stole that gun from Hilda's office?" I asked. "And that's how Pupik's gun ended up killing Maria?"

"I don't know, Ida, but for now, as we're proceeding on the assumption Pupik didn't do it, that's our best possibility, isn't it?"

I had to agree. If that was the gun that killed Maria, and Pupik is telling the truth, it must have been taken from the shelf on which I'd seen it.

About an hour later Mrs. K received a telephone call from Margaret. Pupik had given her a list he'd prepared with the names of people he could remember who had come to his office during the time between our being there and the Purim party. Mrs. K made some notes with her pencil, then thanked Margaret and hung up the phone. I glanced over her shoulder.

"It's not a long list," I said, "and not surprising Maria is on it."

"Yes," Mrs. K said. She was staring into the distance now, holding the list. She said, more to herself than to me, "Now, I wonder…."

I didn't find out what she wondered, because just then the phone rang again. This time it was the shoe repair store to tell Mrs. K her new heels were ready. When she hung up, we saw it was time to go to dinner, and that was all of the murder case we talked about that day.

Nu, enough is enough.

Chapter 31

The next morning before breakfast, Mrs. K seemed awfully excited, at least for her.

"So what is it that's on your mind?" I asked her as we walked down the hallway. "You seem pleased about something, like the cat that ate the … the little bird."

"The canary. And I am pleased," she said. "I'll tell you about it after breakfast. We have a busy day ahead."

Naturally, I could hardly wait for breakfast to be over to find out what was on Mrs. K's mind. I think I gulped my orange juice in a most unladylike way, and I ate my bagel with a *shmeer* so fast I gave myself heartburn. *Oy,* I should know better.

After Mrs. K and I had finished eating and said some pleasant words to our table companions, we found an empty corner of the lounge where to sip our tea and talk.

"So tell me already," I said.

"Well, Ida, last evening I made a list of all the information we have gathered, and I checked off those things that seemed to me most significant, and also of those things that have, shall we say, puzzled me along the way."

"What do you mean, puzzled you?"

"Oh, things that seemed important, but I couldn't quite figure out why. Where they fit into the picture."

"And did making this list help you to be less puzzled?"

"It did. I finally had a theory that made sense. At least to me. One that ties up all those loose ends. I also obtained Hilda's phone number from Marilyn at the front desk."

"Hilda? Why did you need Hilda's number?"

"Because I wanted to corroborate Pupik's story that he told us, about the gun. That's a crucial part of the puzzle."

"So what did she say?"

"I asked her whether Pupik had ever given her a gun in a shoebox. She seemed very surprised I would be asking, but she said yes, and her story was exactly the same as Pupik's."

"Then Pupik was telling the truth," I said, "and he didn't have the gun that killed Maria." But then something occurred to me.

"But even if Pupik gave the gun to Hilda like he told us," I said, "what if he took back the gun himself?"

"Very good, Ida," Mrs. K said. "You can see that Pupik is still not, as they say, off the hook." I pictured Pupik dangling on a hook like a fish, wriggling and trying to get free. I'm ashamed to say I found the picture amusing. Guilty or innocent, Pupik is still Pupik.

"So at least half his story is true," Mrs. K said. I stopped picturing Pupik and paid attention. "And it fits in with my theory."

"All right already. So tell me what is this theory of yours."

"I will, on our way to the police headquarters. I want to explain it to the police so they will think twice about proceeding with this trial of Pupik before they've looked carefully at other possibilities. I've made an appointment for this afternoon with that Porter woman."

I didn't like the sound of that. "Can't we go and see Inspector Corcoran himself?" I asked. "Him we can talk to. Her I'm not so sure."

"I tried that, Ida, but just like last time, Corcoran said we need to talk to Porter, because she's in charge of the case now. So we will do as he said."

I supposed we would, but I didn't have a good feeling about it.

****

Mrs. K and I took a taxi to the downtown police headquarters where we had met with Inspector Corcoran many times in the past. On the way I asked her about something that had been bothering me since we found out that Maria's husband John wrote the blackmail note to Pupik. Maybe for once I was one step ahead of Mrs. K. Or at least not a step behind, as usual.

"Rose," I said, "before you tell me what your new theory is, I want to ask: If John Cartwright knew about Maria's *shtuping* Pupik, would that not give him an excellent motive for killing her? Better than anyone else we've considered? So is he the person you now suspect?"

"That's a good question, Ida, and I've thought about it too, but I don't think the husband is the killer. Let's look at the sequence of events: The blackmail note was written after Maria was killed, of course. If Cartwright shot Maria, it was just lucky for him Pupik came along and picked up the gun. He obviously couldn't have planned it that way. But now that Pupik is being held for the murder, Cartwright has every incentive to see him convicted. He would want to tell the police about Pupik's affair with Maria in order to make that conviction more likely, rather than withhold it, even for ten thousand dollars."

I let that circulate in my brain for a minute. I thought I saw a problem with Mrs. K's reasoning (a rare occurrence).

"But Rose, couldn't he tell the police anyway, once he gets the money from Pupik? It's not like he is turning over to Pupik some object for his payment, so now Pupik has it and Cartwright doesn't. He makes only a promise not to tell the police, and he can easily break it."

"A very good point, Ida. Let's see where it takes us. Pupik pays Cartwright, Cartwright then double-crosses, I think is the term, Pupik and tells the police anyway. He probably would then have to testify against Pupik at his trial. Pupik would then know, if he hadn't figured it out already, that Cartwright is likely the one who blackmailed him, and that he broke his promise."

"I see," I said, because I suddenly did. "Pupik might be convicted of murder, but he would make sure Cartwright went to jail for blackmail."

"Exactly. And Cartwright would realize that once the police knew about the affair—remember Cartwright thinks only he knows—and that Cartwright was aware of it, they might see that it gave Cartwright just as good a motive as Pupik, if not better, and they might turn their attention to him as a suspect. No, if he was the killer, I doubt very much he would also be the blackmailer."

"And vice versa, yes?"

"Yes. And then there is the question of how Cartwright would have obtained Pupik's pistol. He's not likely to have been in Pupik's office, and he's not on the list Pupik gave us. So under the circumstances I don't think it probable that John Cartwright is our killer, much as it might simplify things if he were."

I can't say I was not disappointed that I hadn't figured out the solution to the case, but I couldn't argue with Mrs. K's reasoning.

Once we had disposed of John Cartwright, Mrs. K began to explain her new theory about the case.

"I don't think we accounted for everyone who had a motive and an opportunity," she said. She was about to tell me who it was she suspected, but just then we arrived at police headquarters. I wanted her to continue, but Mrs. K patted my hand and said, "Patience, Ida, you must trust me on this."

"Trust I can do," I said. "Patience is another matter."

****

We walked into the police headquarters building. Unlike Corcoran, the Porter woman was not in a nice office with windows and a door, but she was behind a desk in a big room on the third floor, with several other desks and a lot of noise from other officers—I assume they were officers, though most of them were not wearing uniforms—talking to each other or on the telephone.

When we approached her desk, Porter looked up from something she was reading. She gave us what you might call a weak smile—perhaps it was the best she could do—and said, "Hello, Mrs. Kaplan, Mrs. Berkowitz. Please sit down." It was the most polite we had heard her speak at one time since we met her. Perhaps this was progress.

There was only one chair available in front of the desk, so I dragged another one over from the desk next door, the officer behind the desk giving me a look like I was stealing it. Maybe they're trained to look like that. Anyway, soon we were seated, and Porter said, "I assume you came to talk about the Pupik case."

"That's right," Mrs. K said. "I wanted …"

But she didn't get any further, as Porter interrupted.

"I think I can save us all a lot of time, Mrs. Kaplan. I've looked at all the evidence and I've interviewed all the persons involved, and there is simply no doubt in my mind that we have the right suspect." So progress this was not.

"But there are still many unanswered questions," Mrs. K said, "and I have a theory …"

"Yes, I'm sure you do," Porter said, interrupting again. "And I know you like to play amateur detective there at the Cohen Home. But as I said, there is really no doubt here. We have the killer discovered standing over his victim. He's holding his own gun, which is still smoking, so to speak. It would be difficult to find a more open-and-shut case, except perhaps if someone had actually seen him fire the gun. But you can't have everything, can you?"

"And what about the fact the gun hadn't been in Mr. Pupik's possession for some weeks before, but was in his secretary's office?" Mrs. K asked.

"Yes, yes, he told us that. But even if it's true, there was nothing preventing him from retrieving it when he wanted to use it. We checked with the gun shop he said he was taking it to, and they never received it. No, that story doesn't change anything."

It was interesting how the same facts, the same story Pupik told us and the police, seemed to us to help him, and seemed to the police—or at least to this police person—to make no difference.

I was about to make a protest, but Mrs. K put her hand on my arm to keep me quiet. She then said to Porter,

"Yes, I see you aren't interested in listening to us or considering another possibility. I thank you for your time."

She stood up, indicated I should follow, and we walked out of the big room.

I was glad to leave the noise behind. And even more glad to leave Missy Porter behind.

****

"So, Rose, what are we going to do now?" I asked. "Are you giving up?"

She gave me a look, like I was *meshugeh*. "Of course not," she said. "The Porter woman might be right, or she might not. But we aren't going to let a man be tried for murder without at least giving him every benefit of the doubt."

"But I wish it were a nicer man than Pupik we were giving the benefit," I said.

"Now, Ida, we must be like Mr. Sherlock Holmes. He said he would never approach a case with a prejudice, but would always 'follow docilely where the facts lead me.' That is what we must do."

"*Nu,* so where is it these facts are leading us?"

"To Inspector Corcoran's office, Ida."

"But I thought you said …"

"I said Corcoran told us to talk with the Porter woman. We have talked to Porter. She didn't want to listen. So now we will talk to Corcoran."

"And if he doesn't want to listen either?"

Mrs. K straightened her shoulders and turned toward the elevator.

"Don't worry, Ida," she said. "He will listen."

Chapter 32

We took the elevator down to the second floor, where was Inspector Corcoran's office. I recognized his secretary from the last time we'd been there, and when she looked up she seemed to recognize us. She smiled.

"You must be here to see Inspector Corcoran," she said. "Is he expecting you?"

"That depends," Mrs. K said. "If he suspected we would get nowhere with his assistant, he probably anticipated we would be knocking on his door next. But no, we don't have an appointment, if that's what you mean."

Still smiling—and such a lovely smile she had—she got up from her desk, went over to Corcoran's door, and quietly knocked. She then opened the door and said something we couldn't hear to someone we couldn't see, I assume the Inspector. There was a muffled reply, and then she backed out of the office, closed the door, and returned to her desk.

"The Inspector is quite busy right now," she said, "but he can give you about five minutes before his next appointment."

Mrs. K looked at me, then back to the secretary. "*Nu,* five minutes is not enough, but it's better than nothing. Come, Ida, we'll take what we can get."

The secretary again knocked on Corcoran's door, then opened it to let us go in and closed it behind us. And there was Inspector Corcoran, sleeves rolled up, papers in several piles on his desk, obviously very busy. But as soon as we entered he stood up, smiled, and shook hands with us, indicating we should sit. We sat.

"I always am glad to see you ladies," Corcoran said, "but I hope you'll understand that I'm in something of a hurry. I have an important appointment in a few minutes. So if we can get right to the point, I assume you're here about the shooting at the Home. And you know I've assigned that case to Sergeant Porter. Have you talked with her?"

"It's more that she has talked to us," Mrs. K said. "She didn't want to listen to what we had to say, only to tell us the case was solved and there was nothing further that needed to be done."

Corcoran appeared to be thinking this over. He said, "I see. Well, she may be correct about that, but if I've learned anything from our previous …uh … encounters, it's not to dismiss anything you have to say without giving you every opportunity to back it up. Unfortunately, I simply don't have the time to listen right now, as I'm already late for an appointment, and then my wife and I are leaving for a short vacation, until next Tuesday. I'm going to the airport right from my appointment. But I promise to give you all the time you need when I return.

"Meanwhile, please keep in mind that we can only proceed on the evidence we have, not on speculation, no matter how clever it might be. If you can come up with some solid evidence to back up your theory, whatever it is, I will personally see that it's followed up thoroughly. But in the meantime, there's really nothing I can do except allow Sergeant Porter to proceed as she sees fit."

Mrs. K was silent. She just nodded to indicate she understood. We would have to have more than a theory. We would have to find evidence. The police had a lot of evidence: a "smoking gun," as Porter said.

What could we find to top that?

****

"So what do we do now?" I asked Mrs. K. We were back at the Home, sitting in the lounge as usual and having a cup of tea. But it was not usual in any other way, as you'll see.

"Well, Ida, Inspector Corcoran said he needs evidence, so evidence he shall have."

"Do you have evidence someone other than Pupik shot Maria?" If she did, she hadn't bothered to tell me.

"Not yet, but I plan to."

****

It was the next morning, Saturday morning to be exact, and I was anxious to know whether Mrs. K had come up with how she was going to get the evidence Corcoran wanted.

As we were walking to breakfast, I asked her, "So do you have another plan?"

"I do, although I'm afraid it might require another little … little adventure on our part."

I didn't like the sound of that. In the past, Mrs. K's "little adventures" have been either dangerous, illegal, or both. Not that I objected strongly, I suppose, at the time. Sometimes it's just what has to be done.

"So tell me, Rose. Does this latest 'adventure' involve my niece Sara's friend the lady burglar?" At least twice in the past we've had to call on this lady, whose name is Florence.

"You're almost reading my mind, Ida. But no, I

hope we won't need that lady's services again just yet."

"Just yet, you say. So who will be having this adventure? Not us, I hope."

Mrs. K laughed. "I certainly hope not," she said.

"So who then," I asked again.

"You shall see. Meanwhile, perhaps you'll take a little taxi ride with me tomorrow morning?"

"A taxi ride to where?"

"Back to Pupik's house."

I didn't ask Mrs. K why we were going there, and she didn't seem inclined to volunteer the information. *Nu,* I would find out soon enough.

Snooping with Mrs. K is a little like watching one of those serials on TV. If you want to know how it comes out, you have to tune in next week. Or in this case, tomorrow morning.

Chapter 33

So the next morning Mrs. K and I are taking another yellow taxi, back to Pupik's.

"Does Pupik know we are coming?" I asked as we rattled along a particularly rough surface. Sometimes it seems like they're paving the streets with cobblestones these days, returning them to their former condition a century ago.

"He does, and he's not too pleased about the reason, but that I can't help."

Pupik not pleased? That sounded more like his old self. He must be feeling better, I thought.

We arrived at Pupik's house and knocked on the door. Margaret greeted us and let us in, closing the door behind us. Pupik was standing in the foyer, clearly expecting us, and looking unhappy. He stepped up to Mrs. K without saying anything, took from his pocket what looked like some folded money, two bills to be exact, although I couldn't see the numbers on them. He handed the money to her and she put it in the pocket of her coat.

Pupik giving money to Mrs. K! I thought I'd now seen everything.

He then spoke for the first time since we'd arrived:

"Are you sure this is necessary, Mrs. Kaplan?"

"Yes, I am," Mrs. K said. "It's the only way I can think to find what we're looking for, and I don't have the money to pay for it."

"I understand," Pupik said. "I hope you're right."

"We'll soon know," she said. Then another startling thing: Pupik took Mrs. K's hand in his two and gave it a squeeze. It was like Macy's patting Gimbel's on the back. Or something like that.

Margaret gave us a small smile and let us out.

All the way back to the Home Mrs. K was deep in thought, so I didn't bother her with questions. As usual, she would tell me what she was doing when she was ready.

I hoped it was soon.

****

As soon as we arrived back at Mrs. K's apartment, she walked straight to the phone and made a call. I couldn't hear the conversation, but it was quite short.

"Ida," she said after she'd hung up the phone, "do you still have that little camera you were planning to give to your grandson for his birthday?"

"Yes," I said. "It isn't yet his birthday, so it's still in a drawer."

"Good. How would you like a chance to … to test it out before you give it to him?"

"How do you mean 'test it out'? Don't they do that at the factory?"

"I suppose so, but another time won't hurt."

I thought about this. Something wasn't *kosher* here. Mrs. K doesn't usually play these games.

"Testing, shmesting," I said. "If you want to borrow the camera just say so."

"All right. May I borrow the camera for the day?"

"Can I ask why?"

"I promise you will know soon. I don't want to

214

explain it twice."

"Twice? You haven't even explained it once. If you—"

But just then there was a knock on Mrs. K's door. I went to answer it and was surprised to see Paula, one of the Home's housekeepers, standing there.

"Did you need something?" I asked her. It's a bit unusual for a housekeeper to come for a visit, except to clean an apartment, which they do when we aren't there.

Paula looked a *bissel* nervous. "Mrs. Kaplan phoned and asked me to come by. I don't know why. I hope I haven't done something wrong."

Just then Mrs. K came to the door and said, "Paula. Thank you for coming. Please come in."

I had no idea why she was there, but obviously Mrs. K had invited her, and I assumed I would shortly know why. She passed into the living room, still looking anxious. Mrs. K sat on the sofa and asked Paula to sit next to her.

Paula is young, perhaps twenty-one, and quite pretty, with short blonde hair and a nice figure. Like I used to have, a lot of matzoh and *schmaltz* ago. But she had never struck me as having a sharp mind. Not the brightest candle in the menorah.

She sat.

"Ida," Mrs. K said, "would you please go and get that camera now? Meanwhile I'll prepare some tea and cookies for us."

As I had already agreed to lend Mrs. K the camera, and I was anxious to find out what she needed it for and what Paula had to do with it, I did as she asked.

When I returned a few minutes later with the camera, Mrs. K and Paula were already sipping their tea.

Paula was still looking quite lost.

I handed the camera to Mrs. K and sat on the chair opposite the sofa. I poured myself a cup of tea and took a biscuit from the plate on the coffee table.

"Paula," Mrs. K said, putting down her cup and turning to her, "I need your assistance. There's a very important item that I believe is in one of the apartments here at the Home. It has to do with the terrible thing that happened during the Purim play."

"Oh, that was just horrible," Paula said, putting her hand over her mouth as one does remembering something unpleasant. "That poor woman."

"Yes," Mrs. K said, "it was horrible. And I've been asked by the police to help them find out who was responsible for it. To do that, I have to know where—in what apartment—a certain item is. That's where you come in."

Paula looked shocked. "Me? I had nothing to do with it. I don't even know what it is you're looking for—"

"Yes, yes, of course not," Mrs. K said, patting Paula on the hand. "I just need your help in finding it. You're one of the people who clean our rooms every day, while we're at breakfast or lunch, is that right?"

"Yes," Paula said.

"So you have to look around each apartment to see that everything is clean and in order."

"Well, yes, although just enough to see what needs to be cleaned."

"Of course. So since you are there already, and looking around already, you might be able to see if a certain object is lying around, yes?"

"I suppose so."

"And you could tell me if you saw that object there?"

"I guess I could, but that seems to be ... to be invading someone's privacy, doesn't it?" Perhaps Paula was a little sharper than I'd thought.

"Not at all," Mrs. K assured her, sounding quite certain. "Has anyone ever told you that you can't mention anything you see in an apartment?"

Paula hesitated. "Well ... no, I guess not."

"Yes, so it's not, as you say, invading anyone's privacy."

"So you just want me to tell you if I see this ... this object in an apartment."

Here things got more complicated.

"Yes," said Mrs. K, "but also I would like you to open a few drawers to see if it's there as well."

Paula looked shocked. "Oh, I couldn't do that," she said, sounding as if she'd been asked to steal the crown jewels. "That definitely would be wrong."

Mrs. K assumed a more confidential tone. "Paula, I know ordinarily this would seem to be, well, you might say snooping. Which is not usually a proper thing to do. But remember I've been asked by the police to do this, so in a way you're doing it for the police, to help solve a terrible murder."

Paula was silent, obviously thinking over what Mrs. K had said. I was thinking it over too, and it didn't sound like what I remembered the police asking us to do.

Mrs. K then said, "And I'll give you one hundred dollars to do this little thing for us."

That definitely got Paula's attention. And of course now I knew exactly why Pupik had given that money to Mrs. K.

Paula looked up at Mrs. K. "A hundred dollars? That's a lot of money."

"Yes, it is," Mrs. K said. "And it's for doing something quite simple that will do no harm to anyone."

Anyone except the person who killed Maria, I thought.

Paula was silent again, so Mrs. K took one of the two bills out of her pocket. I could now see that it was a fifty-dollar bill.

"I'll give you this now, and when you've done your little … your little job, you'll get the other fifty dollars. Is that fair?"

Paula took the money, if a bit uncertainly.

"But what if I don't find what you're looking for? What if it isn't there?"

"You will get the other fifty dollars anyway. It's not your fault if I … if the police are mistaken about this object being there."

Paula took another minute to think, staring at the fifty-dollar bill in her hand, which must have represented quite a nice bonus for her, before saying, "Okay. Tell me what you're looking for." I was anxious to know too.

Mrs. K thanked Paula and squeezed her hand, then said, "Do you know what a holster is?"

"You mean what cowboys carry their guns in, in the western movies?"

Mrs. K laughed. "Yes, I suppose they do. Well, this is a much smaller holster, for a smaller gun, and it isn't what any respectable cowboy would be seen with. Maybe a cowgirl. It has several jewels on it, in different colors. You can't miss it."

"I see," Paula said, twisting the bill in her hand so hard I thought it might drip green ink.

Now Mrs. K took the camera I had brought and handed it to Paula.

"Take this with you next time you do up the rooms, and if you should find that holster, just take a picture of it. Don't move it or touch it, just take the picture. Do you understand?"

Paula took the camera and nodded.

"Good," Mrs. K said. "Here is a list of the four rooms I'd like you to check. Three apartments and another room." She handed a piece of paper to Paula, who took it and shoved it into her pocket.

Mrs. K patted Paula's hand again.

"So now let's have some more tea."

Chapter 34

After Paula had left the apartment, I poured myself a third cup of tea (I would be visiting the toilet often that day) and said to Mrs. K, "Rose, there are just a few things I need you to clear up for me."

"Certainly, Ida. What are they?"

"Well, to begin, since when did Corcoran, or 'the police,' tell you to snoop in the residents' apartments?"

Mrs. K looked just a little sheepish.

"Okay, maybe he didn't say exactly that. But he did tell me to find evidence of my theory, and that's what I'm doing, am I not?"

"Hmm. I suppose so. Still …"

"Good. So what's the next question?"

That was clearly as far as that line of questioning was going, so I asked, "*Nu,* what makes you think whoever took Pupik's gun and shot Maria with it would be keeping the holster, which like you say is evidence they did it?"

"That's a very good question, Ida. I have a theory. If the gun were just in that old shoe box you saw in Pupik's office, I'm sure the killer would have burned it or thrown it in the trash right away. But think about the holster, which itself is quite beautiful, and valuable. Knowing the people I have in mind, or anyone for that matter, they wouldn't just throw away such an item, even to protect themselves."

"I see your point, but what do you think they would do with it?"

"I think they would keep it for at least a while, and then when they thought it was safe—perhaps after Pupik had been convicted of the murder—they would find a way to sell it, or at least take out the jewels and sell them."

I thought about this. It was certainly possible, but what you would call a longshot, and I said as much to Mrs. K.

"Yes, I know," she said. "But I think it's worth a try."

"And what if this person we're looking for doesn't live at the Home, like maybe Naomi or her brother? Or Maria's husband?"

"We'll then have to think of a way to snoop in their home as well. And for that we may need the assistance of your Sara's friend, after all. In any case, I think it's worth trying here. And besides, it's Pupik who's paying for it, not me."

"So I saw. How did you get him to give you a hundred dollars?"

"I just explained what I needed it for, and that it should be worth the gamble—and worth permitting Paula to go a *bissel* beyond her usual duties—to prove his innocence."

"If he's innocent," I said.

"Exactly. And since he insists he is, and since he can well afford the money, he couldn't very well refuse, could he?"

And that explained that.

****

It was two days later that Mrs. K asked me to come

221

by her apartment, and there I found her with Paula, who was holding the camera in one hand and the other fifty dollars in the other.

This time Paula was looking quite pleased with herself. And Mrs. K was looking even more pleased.

"Ida," Mrs. K said, "Paula has found what we were looking for. And she took a picture. We'll make an appointment with Inspector Corcoran and bring him our evidence."

Paula handed Mrs. K the camera, and she handed it to me. "Keep this safe until we need it," she said. I promised to do just that.

****

The next day we took a taxi to police headquarters and again sat down with Inspector Corcoran. Mrs. K had explained to me where the holster had been found, and what she thought had occurred. I was still skeptical that the police would listen, but I was looking forward to what Corcoran would say.

But we did not see just Corcoran. When we were shown into his office, there was the Porter woman, sitting to one side with her ever-present notebook poised to take down every word. Or maybe just the words she wanted to take down.

"Good morning, ladies. You know Sergeant Porter, of course. I thought since we're pretty much at the conclusion of this case, and Sergeant Porter has been in charge of the investigation, she should be here to listen to what you have to say, and of course to add her own comments."

"Yes, of course," Mrs. K said, and she gave Porter a smile. But I'm sure she didn't mean it.

"First, I apologize for not having time for you the

last time you were here. It was simply not possible to squeeze you in just then. But I'm ready to listen now, so let's get right down to it," Corcoran said. "The last time we talked, you said you had an interesting theory, and I suggested you make sure you have evidence to back it up. I understand you've found what you consider evidence, so why don't you present that to us now?"

Here Porter spoke up for the first time. From her tone, I suspected Inspector Corcoran had had a word with her, as they say, perhaps suggesting she could be more courteous, and more patient, with members of the public. Especially members of the public who had saved the Inspector from some unfortunate mistakes in the past.

"Would you mind, Mrs. Kaplan," she said, "first telling us who it is you suspect is the guilty party, if not Mr. Pupik? It might make it easier to follow your story. Much as we all enjoy the living room scenes in the movies, where the detective waits until the last second to name the killer," and at this we all laughed, because we all did enjoy those stories, "in a real case like this, the better we understand where you're going, the better we can evaluate your conclusion when you get there."

Gevalt, it was the longest speech I had heard Porter speak since we met her. But I had to admit that it seemed like a reasonable request, and I suppose Mrs. K agreed, because she said, "I think you're right. This is not a game or a movie. In my opinion, Maria was not killed by Pupik, or her husband, or Naomi, but it was someone in Naomi's family."

"You mean her brother, Barry?" Corcoran said.

"No, no, not the brother, and not the husband. No, it wasn't Naomi.

"It was her mother, Miriam Blumenthal."

Chapter 35

Inspector Corcoran looked more than surprised. He seemed to be trying to keep from laughing, or at least smiling at Mrs. K's suggestion. Porter, to her credit, didn't change expression, but merely made another note in her book.

To be quite honest, when Mrs. K had finally told me her theory, I had almost the same reaction as Corcoran. However, I know Mrs. K well enough not to be so quick to doubt her. If she makes such a statement as this, she has thought it through.

Corcoran composed himself, smiled encouragingly at both of us, and now stood up from his desk. I thought it was to indicate the interview was over, so ridiculous was Mrs. K's suggestion. But this wasn't so, because he said, "If you'll excuse me, I'll get a cup of coffee. I have a feeling this will be a rather long presentation. Would any of you ladies like a cup?"

We declined—I very seldom drink coffee, nor does Mrs. K—and so did Porter. It would probably interfere with her note-taking. Corcoran went for his coffee, and when he had returned and sat back down, he took a sip and asked Mrs. K please to continue. Mrs. K cleared her throat and began:

"As we all know, Maria Cartwright was killed by a gun owned by Mr. Pupik, the manager of the Home, and Pupik was found holding the gun over Maria's body."

We all nodded. So far, no argument.

"We also know from Miriam, who was being attended by her employee Maria, that she was in the back of the kitchen ready to taste some fresh-baked *hamantaschen*. From there she saw the shooting, but the shooter was wearing a mask so she didn't see who he— or she—was."

More nodding.

"Of course, there must always be found both a motive and an opportunity for a crime. The opportunity was there for anyone who attended the Purim party, which was most of the residents and a few others. As for motive, Ida and I already knew about Maria's fooling around, at least with Pupik, and it was easy to guess he was not the only one. This gave a motive not only to Pupik, who she—what would you say—dumped? Anyway, not only he had the motive, but no doubt there were others she had had affairs with, plus their wives if they found out. And in fact we later learned about several such people."

Porter was writing all this down. Kept her from being bored, I was thinking.

"Would you care to tell us who those others are?" Corcoran said.

"Only if later you think it necessary, if that's okay," Mrs. K said. Corcoran nodded.

"So we had to narrow down the field, so to speak. Too many possible suspects. It occurred to me that when it came to opportunity, our killer not only had to be at the party, but he—or she—had to have had access to Pupik's gun. Apparently the gun was in Pupik's secretary's office for some time, waiting to be repaired."

Corcoran interrupted: "Are you sure of that, Mrs.

Kaplan?"

"Ida and I saw it there; or at least Ida did, didn't you, Ida?"

I nodded. I was glad to have a bit of a part in this movie scene.

"And Hilda, Pupik's secretary, told us the same story."

"I see," Corcoran said. "Yes, she told us the same. Please go on."

"Thank you. I asked myself, who would most likely have had access to Pupik's office during the time the box with the gun was there? And that too narrowed down the possible suspects. I won't bore you with the list, but it was not long."

"I would imagine not," Corcoran said.

"And all this time," Mrs. K continued, "I kept in mind two of Mr. Sherlock Holmes' most important statements."

"You mean the one about the dog in the night?" Corcoran asked, smiling.

"No, not that one. Although possibly it applies as well. No, Mr. Holmes said that 'it's a mistake to theorize in advance of the facts,' because one will 'begin to twist facts to suit theories instead of theories to suit facts.' I believe that once we all saw Pupik holding that smoking gun, which certainly was a fact, everyone began to fit that and whatever new facts they found to the theory that Pupik was guilty."

"That seems somewhat unfair, Mrs. Kaplan," Corcoran protested. "What other theory fits the facts we have, including the fact of Mr. Pupik holding the gun?"

"Yes, I'm getting to that," Mrs. K said. "Mr. Holmes also said, 'the world is full of obvious things which nobody ever observes,' or words to that effect. I think he meant that we look but we don't always see. Mr. Holmes always examined the world around him closely. Even with a magnifying glass he's often shown. Let me tell you what I observed but did not, at first, see.

"When Ida and I went to the back of the kitchen to help Miriam, she said she had seen the shooting from a place several feet away from where we found her. I went over to that spot and looked out toward the front of the kitchen. But when I bent down to the level that Miriam would have been, sitting in her wheelchair, I could no longer see to where Maria was lying, because the oven was in the way. That bothered me at the time, but it didn't immediately occur to me what this meant. But later, when I put it together with other facts, I understood."

Porter was writing furiously, and Corcoran was leaning forward, his chin resting on his hand. He was clearly interested.

Corcoran said, "What 'other facts' do you mean, Mrs. Kaplan?"

"Well, at first it meant nothing to me when Miriam said she had gone to the back of the kitchen to sample the warm *hamantaschen.* Who wouldn't want to do the same? But many days later, as Ida and I were sitting in the lounge, I again observed something that didn't immediately … what is it … didn't immediately register with me, not until later.

"Ida, do you remember when we were served cookies with our tea, and we noticed that some of the others in the lounge were being served glutenless—no, I think they call it gluten-free—cookies?"

I said yes, I did remember. I also now saw where Mrs. K was going with this. The lightbulb, it was going on over my head.

"Well, one of the residents I saw being served the gluten-free cookies was Miriam. I don't think anyone prefers a gluten-free cookie if they have a choice of a ... a glutonous one? You know what I mean. And then I remembered Naomi saying her mother never had *hamantaschen* in the house when she was a girl. It probably was because it didn't agree with her. In any case, it would not now, because she stays away from things with gluten."

Porter looked up now, and she was kind of staring into space as if thinking about what Mrs. K had said, and then she returned to scribbling her notes.

I was remembering how Naomi had said her mother was pretty good at acting in the Purim play as a child. She seems to still have that acting talent.

Inspector Corcoran said, "Those are very interesting observations on your part, Mrs. Kaplan. And yes, they are evidence, if circumstantial. But they're hardly sufficient to prove that Mrs. Blumenthal shot Maria Cartwright. You understand, I'm sure, that a charge like that requires much more than proving someone lied about whether they saw the murder, or why they were in the back of the kitchen. It could have been for many reasons, only one of which is that she shot Maria, and that one is probably the most unlikely."

Mrs. K nodded. She didn't seem upset by what seemed to be Corcoran's dismissal of her observations as insufficient. I'm sure she realized it herself.

"I agree completely, Inspector," she said. "What these observations did was to raise a suspicion, at least in my mind if not in yours, a suspicion that required me to take the next step and ask myself, did Miriam also have the opportunity and motive to shoot Maria, her helper?

"Of course, she was in the kitchen alone with Maria when she was shot—well, alone except for the killer if it was not her—so she had the opportunity."

"Wait a minute," Corcoran said. "You said, correctly I think, that opportunity means not only the opportunity to shoot Maria, but also the opportunity to acquire Pupik's gun. How do you account for that?"

"That's a good question," Mrs. K said, not seeming perturbed at all. "It almost had to be someone who visited Pupik's office while the gun was there, and while Hilda, Pupik's secretary, was not. As I already mentioned, Ida and I did so, and Ida discovered the gun because she was doing a little innocent snooping while I was busy at the office door."

I wasn't sure I liked that description, but I let it go. Besides, it was true.

"But we also know that Maria was a frequent visitor to Pupik, and I'm sure at least some of the time she came there with Miriam, on some excuse, leaving her in the outer office while she *shmoosed*—or maybe fooled around—with Pupik in his office. In such a case it would be easy for Miriam to do as Ida did while she was waiting, snoop around, open the box, see the gun, and just take it out and conceal it under her robe."

Corcoran didn't look or sound convinced. "Hmm. Okay, let's pass that and go on to motive."

"As for motive, that was more difficult for me to understand. Why would Miriam want to kill the person who was so valuable to her, who helped her to get around, took her to movies and to the park, and, it turns out, took her gambling? And that, I think, is where we might find the motive."

"Gambling gave her a motive to murder her helper?" Corcoran asked. "How do you figure that?"

"Not just gambling. Let's not forget, Inspector," Mrs. K said, "that well before Maria was killed, I'd been asked by Miriam's daughter Naomi to investigate something else about Maria Cartwright: Where Maria was taking Miriam, because she was worried that Maria was taking advantage of her mother and trying to get money from her, to the exclusion of Naomi and the other members of the family."

"Yes, but you told me Mrs. Blumenthal was too mentally unstable to resist. I take it that means she wouldn't realize what Maria was doing."

"That's true. That's what Naomi seemed to think. But I'm not so sure it's accurate. First, Naomi told me her mother used to deal very harshly with people who tried to take advantage of her, and I believe she still has a lot of that spirit. Miriam told Naomi not to worry about her, that she could take care of herself. It's therefore quite possible that she realized Maria was taking advantage of her and took a drastic way to stop it. And it's also possible she suspected Naomi's husband of having an affair with Maria and that too would provide a motive, to protect or avenge her daughter. But I admit motive is still a bit of an open question."

Corcoran held up a hand like a policeman holding up traffic—as maybe he had to do when he first joined the police force—and said, "So let's see where we now are: You've found that Mrs. Blumenthal apparently lied about her actions in the kitchen following Maria's death. You think there might be a motive for Mrs. Blumenthal to harm Maria, but you're not sure. I'm sorry, but your case is still pretty weak, Mrs. Kaplan."

As he said this, I saw Porter flipping pages of her notebook back and forth, like she was looking for something.

"I agree it needs more evidence, and I think I've found it," Mrs. K said. And here she took out the little camera she had borrowed from me, turned it on, and handed it to Corcoran.

"If you'll look at the little screen on the back of this camera, you'll find a very interesting picture," she said.

Corcoran took the camera and looked. Softly he whistled.

"Is this the holster that Pupik's gun had been in?" he asked Mrs. K.

"Yes. I showed the picture to Pupik yesterday, and he identified it." And then she added, like an afterthought, "I didn't tell him where I got the picture, if you're wondering."

Corcoran laughed. "I'm sure you followed correct police procedures, Mrs. Kaplan. So now the important question: Where did you take this picture?"

Mrs. K seemed to fidget a little before answering, as if she didn't want to say. But she said.

"I didn't actually take this picture, and I'm afraid I can't tell you who did. But I know where it was taken, and when: It was taken in Miriam Blumenthal's apartment, yesterday. If you look closely, you'll see the holster is in a lingerie drawer, partially covered by a … a …"

"A brassiere," Corcoran said. "Yes, I can see that. But if that's the holster, and if you, or whoever you got to do your dirty work, found it in Mrs. Blumenthal's drawer …"

"Then we have a whole new case, and it looks like Pupik may be innocent after all."

You probably think this last was said by Mrs. K. But it was not. To my great surprise and I'm sure Mrs. K's, it was Porter who said this, looking up from her notepad.

"I'm not sure I would go that far at this point, Cynthia" Corcoran said. He's always the cautious one. But Porter didn't back down. With her, apparently, things are either black or white.

"It's all here, Inspector," she said. "It all adds up. And when I look back at the interviews we've had with both Pupik and the other residents, it's all pretty consistent with Mrs. Kaplan's theory."

I couldn't believe what I was hearing. It was Porter, who we thought was being so rigid and unwilling to consider any other suspect than Pupik, who now seemed to be convinced they had been mistaken. All the time she was scribbling in her notepad, she apparently was also thinking about how the pieces of the case fit together.

Who knew?

Corcoran looked at Porter for quite a while before scratching his chin and saying, "Yes, well, we'll have to open a whole new phase of this investigation, won't we?" Then, turning to face Mrs. K and me, he said, "Is there anything else you'd like to add to what you've told us? Any further evidence we, uh, overlooked?"

He sounded a *bissel* frustrated, and to be honest, I can't blame him. Even for a policeman who is as honest and anxious to be fair as I know Corcoran is, it has to be deflating to think he has a case neatly sewed up, only to have a couple of old ladies come along and rip out all the stitches.

We shook our heads.

"Ladies," Corcoran said, standing up, "I really do appreciate your having brought all this to our attention, and you can be sure we'll follow it up. As Sergeant Porter has said, it does begin to look like we could have the wrong man. But you'll have to leave the matter with us, and trust us to ... to reach the right conclusion."

We both nodded. What else could we do?

"Meanwhile," Corcoran went on, "please keep all of this to yourselves. Any hint that we are taking this ... this different approach to the case might cause irreparable harm. Do you understand?"

"Of course," Mrs. K said. "We understand, and we'll be careful not to say anything."

"And may I hang onto this camera for a little while?"

"Sure," I said, "only be careful with it—it's a present for my grandson."

"Thank you. I'll be very careful. Now if you'll excuse us, Sergeant Porter and I have a lot of work to do, and quickly."

And that was that.

Or so we thought.

Chapter 36

Mrs. K and I returned to the Home, satisfied that we had helped a man who had been wrongly charged with murder escape a punishment he didn't deserve.

Even if he is a *momzer*. Or has been.

As we were walking down the hall toward our rooms, who did we see coming toward us, pushing herself along in her wheelchair, but Miriam Blumenthal! After we just got through telling the police that she was the one who killed Maria.

An awkward situation, was it not?

"Hello, ladies," Miriam said. "On your way to lunch?"

"Not quite yet," Mrs. K said, and we both did our best to act natural.

We probably should have left it at that, but Mrs. K added, "We haven't had a chance to tell you how sorry we are about … well, about what happened with Maria."

I expected Miriam to say something like, "Yes, it was quite a shock." Instead she surprised us by saying, "Good riddance, if you ask me. She was a real *nafkeh*." A whore? Where did this come from?

"But you seemed to get along quite well with her," I said.

"Yes, that was before …. But let's not speak ill of the dead, shall we? Let's just say we're all now better off."

It was a little late not to speak ill of Maria, Miriam having done so in no uncertain terms. But Mrs. K and I just nodded, wished Miriam a good day, and continued on our way.

****

It wasn't until three days later that we heard again from Corcoran. He asked us to come to his office, and of course we did so as soon as we were able. We wanted to know what his further investigation had turned up. I assumed, of course, it had corroborated Mrs. K's theory.

What we learned was that it turned up quite a bit.

"Well, ladies," Corcoran began after Mrs. K and I were again seated in front of his desk, Porter again taking notes on the side, "I'm forced to admit you have again steered us in the right direction."

"So you agree that it was Miriam Blumenthal who shot Maria, and not Pupik?" Mrs. K said.

Corcoran leaned back in his chair and said, "Well, yes and no." Yes and no? What kind of an answer was that?

"Yes, we've cleared Mr. Pupik. I'm sure he'll be most grateful to you for that."

"We're glad to hear that, Inspector," Mrs. K said. "And the no?"

"No, it wasn't Miriam Blumenthal who shot Maria Cartwright."

Mrs. K and I just looked at each other, and together we turned toward Corcoran and said like in a chorus, "Not Miriam?"

"Yes. I mean no. I'll let Sergeant Porter explain, as it was she who led the investigation."

Corcoran looked over at Porter, who put down her notebook, turned to us, and actually smiled! Things were getting more *meshugeh* by the minute.

"After our meeting with you the other day," Porter said, "we quickly obtained a search warrant for Miriam Blumenthal's apartment, as we were afraid she might dispose of that holster before we could recover it, especially if she noticed that someone had opened her drawer. We searched her apartment the next day."

"And did you find the holster?" Mrs. K asked.

"We certainly did. And we found something else."

"What was that?" I asked. Although of course this was unnecessary, as she was going to tell us anyway.

"Fingerprints," said Porter.

Corcoran broke in. "Sergeant Porter decided it was a good idea to see what fingerprints were on the holster, as a further way to implicate Mrs. Blumenthal. That is, although finding the holster in her drawer is quite good evidence she put it there, her fingerprints on it would be even better."

Porter continued, "Of course, we did find prints that turned out to be Mrs. Blumenthal's, as well as Mr. Pupik's. But there was another set of fresh prints that we couldn't identify at first. We decided it almost had to be someone in the small number of people we had already interviewed in this case, so we started with them. We easily obtained the fingerprints of two of them who had had a previous arrest, and we were going to have the others fingerprinted. But it turned out we didn't have to.

"One set matched. They belonged to Mrs. Blumenthal's son, Barry."

****

I'm sure both my mouth and Mrs. K's were now hanging open. How did we get this so wrong? Where did Barry come into the picture?

236

Corcoran could see our confusion, and he quickly spoke up.

"Let me clarify that, if I may. What you told us the other day all checked out, and in fact was all correct, all except for the final part, who fired the gun. We got the whole story from Barry. We had brought him in for questioning after finding his prints on the holster—he had been arrested for assault a few years ago, so we had his prints on file—and when it became clear that his mother was implicated and might be charged with the murder, he confessed his part in it."

"As it happens," Porter said, "once she found out we had charged her son, Mrs. Blumenthal tried to take the blame herself and save him. It might have worked, except for one thing."

This was getting better than a mystery story. Even Mr. Sherlock Holmes would be interested.

"And what was that?" Mrs. K asked before I could ask the same thing.

"We re-examined the forensic evidence of the angle of the bullet wound in Mrs. Cartwright's body. We hadn't had occasion to look at that closely before you gave us your theory. Assuming Maria was standing upright when she was shot, and we have no reason to believe she wasn't, the bullet was fired by someone standing in front of her, that is, at her level, and not seated."

"The trajectory was not upward, but more or less level," Corcoran said. "It would have required Mrs. Blumenthal either to stand up in front of her chair, or to hold the gun up at an unnatural angle, to make that kind of a wound."

Corcoran held up a diagram that had been lying on

his desk. I guess it showed what he had just said, although I could not make anything of it. He then continued, "Interestingly enough, had we not found those fingerprints on the holster and been led to Barry Blumenthal, and had we eventually done the forensic work just described to be sure of Miriam Blumenthal's guilt, we might have had to dismiss her as a suspect in the shooting, despite the evidence of the holster. It certainly would have complicated matters considerably."

What is it they say? Wheels within wheels? And who would have expected such a thing from Barry? He may have been a hothead, but otherwise he always seemed like a *mensch,* and we never would have suspected he could shoot someone. It is as the Yiddish saying goes, *In a sheynem epl gefint men a mol a vorem.* In a beautiful apple you sometimes find a worm.

Porter went on to explain that Miriam, once she had been arrested, saw that she might as well tell the police what happened.

"It turns out she hadn't been so fooled by Maria as her daughter Naomi and her family thought, at least not toward the end. It eventually became clear to her that her family was right, that Maria was trying to get at her money. But she thought as long as she didn't sign anything she shouldn't, it wouldn't be a problem, at least until she could find another helper to replace Maria.

"Unfortunately, things then became ugly. Maria saw that Mrs. Blumenthal had developed quite a gambling habit, one she was encouraging by taking her to the casino, as you had observed. Mrs. Blumenthal began losing quite a bit of money, and the last thing she wanted was for her family to find out about it. That's when Maria decided to blackmail her, threatening to tell her family about her gambling habit and losses, unless she paid Maria a large sum of money."

So apparently blackmail ran in the Cartwright family, so to speak. No doubt they were in on this one together.

"And to make matters worse, someone had told Mrs. Blumenthal that Maria was fooling around with her daughter Naomi's husband. Whether or not that was true, it kind of sent Mrs. Blumenthal over the edge, so to speak."

Here Corcoran took over and said, "Apparently, Mrs. Blumenthal found the gun by accident, just as you surmised, and it gave her an idea. She would use it to threaten Maria, to scare her into keeping her mouth shut and keep away from her son-in-law. She confided this in Barry, who was the only person in the family who already knew about her gambling. Barry didn't want his mother to do it. She might get hurt, or Maria might attack her, as she was defenseless unless she actually used the gun on Maria, which she had no intention of doing. So they came up with the idea that Barry would handle the gun, and they would do it right after the Purim party."

So in a strange way, I thought, the possibility that the person who wanted to kill Maria hired someone else to do it, which we had earlier dismissed out of hand, wasn't that far from the truth. Only Miriam got her son's services for free.

Porter again took up the story. "Mrs. Blumenthal says she had a headache and Maria took her into the kitchen to get away from the noise. Barry followed them in and, seeing that they were the only ones there, he decided to get it over with."

"You mean he just decided to shoot her there, with

so many people around?"

"Not exactly," Porter said. "He says he merely wanted to wave the gun around and threaten her, tell her she'd better keep her mouth shut about the gambling. Claims the gun went off accidentally, that he couldn't believe he'd actually shot her."

"Yes," I said, "Pupik said something about the gun having a very delicate trigger. That was one of the things he wanted fixed."

"Did he? So maybe Barry was telling the truth about that. On the other hand, how did bullets get into the gun? We'll see. In any event, he panicked, dropped the gun and fled the kitchen, leaving his mother there with Maria's body."

"The good son," Mrs. K muttered.

"Exactly. And I suppose the rest went just as you surmised. Mrs. Blumenthal got as far away from the body as she could and when you found her, she kind of made up her story as she went along."

Mrs. K shook her head. "And poor Mr. Pupik had the bad luck to be the first to come in and find Maria there, and the bad judgment to pick up the gun. A *shlimazel* and a *schlemiel* all at the same time. Unlucky and stupid, a bad combination.

Everyone was quiet for at least a minute, until Corcoran spoke up.

"Needless to say, Mrs. Kaplan, and you, too, Mrs. Berkowitz, without your putting us on the right track, we might still be directing most of our efforts toward the wrong suspect. You led us to Mrs. Blumenthal, and she led us to Barry. Once again, I owe you both thanks and an apology."

"Why an apology?" Mrs. K asked.

"Because of the, shall we say, uncharitable thoughts I entertained when you first suggested Mrs. Blumenthal's guilt."

"And mine as well," put in Sergeant Porter. "Inspector Corcoran had told me you two were sharper than you … excuse me, he told me you were sharper than one might expect at your … I mean, I just assumed you were not … Let's just say it won't happen again."

"I hope it doesn't have to," Mrs. K said. "No more murders, no more need to think about murderers."

And that would suit me fine too.

Chapter 37

We were back in Mrs. K's apartment, sipping tea of course. It had been a busy day.

Pupik had called to thank us, and especially Mrs. K, for helping to clear him of the murder charge. His wife Margaret got on the phone too and said how relieved she was and how grateful she and her husband were. She invited us both to dine with them next *Shabbes,* and we said we would be pleased to.

Just think of it. Us dining with Pupik. A month earlier even the thought of it would have been *meshugeh.* All of a sudden we're pals. But it beats being enemies.

"I'm still wondering," I said between sips, "what a pretty woman like Maria saw in an old grouch like Pupik. I mean, he has a little money, but he's not so rich as to attract that kind of woman, I wouldn't think."

"I agree, Ida," Mrs. K said. "I don't believe it was money that attracted her. In fact, I don't think it was Pupik at all."

"Not Pupik?"

"Not really. I think she was one of those people who have affairs just because … well, because they can. Men were attracted to her, and it flattered her ego to have them fawn over her. And not to put too fine a point on it, she probably enjoyed having them in her power."

"And in her bed," I added. I don't know why. I hardly ever say things like that.

Mrs. K gave me a look, and I quickly changed the subject. "You were so clever, Rose, to put all those clues together, despite that smoking gun in Pupik's hand."

Mrs. K nodded. "Thank you, Ida. I don't know if it was so clever, but keep in mind this: The trouble with a smoking gun is the possibility of letting the smoke get in your eyes."

"Sherlock Holmes?"

"No. Rose Kaplan."

****

The next morning we were back at our breakfast table, *shmoosing* with Isaac Taubman and Karen Friedlander.

"And so now," Taubman said, "I suppose Pupik will return to being the same old *momzer* as before, now that he's been cleared. I hear he's back in his office today."

"He is," Mrs. K said. "I went to see him. He thanked me and was very nice."

"Oh yes?" Taubman said. "Well, he ought to be. You probably saved his life. Still, do you think his experience will make him any easier to live with for the rest of us?"

Mrs. K looked at me and winked, then turned to Taubman and said, "I don't know if he will be completely reformed. It's unlikely. But we all will benefit, because now I can say this."

She got up.

"Anyone want to try out the new ping pong table?"

A word about the author...

Mark Reutlinger is Professor of Law Emeritus at Seattle University School of Law. He and his wife Analee live in University Place, Washington. Mark's previous novels include the first two "Mrs. Kaplan" mysteries, "MRS. KAPLAN AND THE MATZOH BALL OF DEATH," and "A PAIN IN THE TUCHIS"; "MADE IN CHINA," a political thriller; the caper crime story "MURDER WITH STRINGS ATTACHED"; and romantic suspense novel "SISTER-IN-LAW: VIOLATION, SEDUCTION, and the PRESIDENT OF THE UNITED STATES" (under the pseudonym M. R. Morgan). He is also a reviewer for the New York Journal of Books.

Thank you for purchasing
this publication of The Wild Rose Press, Inc.

For questions or more information
contact us at
info@thewildrosepress.com.

The Wild Rose Press, Inc.
www.thewildrosepress.com